Sherlock Holmes
and the
Mayfair Murders

David Britland

First published in 2011 by
The Irregular Special Press
under the Breese Books imprint
for Baker Street Studios Ltd
Endeavour House
170 Woodland Road, Sawston
Cambridge, CB22 3DX, UK

ISBN: 1-901091-49-X (10 digit)
ISBN: 978-1-901091-49-6 (13 digit)

Cover Concept: Antony J. Richards

Cover Illustrations: Park Lane in Mayfair from an original
contemporary print coloured by Nikki Sims (front) and a psychic
pendulum (back).

Typeset in 8/11/20pt Palatino

About the Author

David Britland is a freelance writer and consultant specialising in all areas of deception, including psychology, magic, the paranormal, con tricks and illusion. He has written books on magic for magicians and worked as a researcher, writer and producer in British television, including Channel 4's alternative magic show, *The Secret Cabaret* and Granada's *James Randi: Psychic Investigator*. For HTV he developed two series of *Something Strange* and a long running Meridian/Anglia series *The Magic & Mystery Show* – this before *The X-Files* turned the paranormal into a bandwagon.

He has also taken a more serious look at the paranormal in several science documentaries developed for Channel 4's *Equinox* series, ranging from the world of the superpsychic to the technology employed in theme parks and a sceptical documentary about hypnosis entitled *The Big Sleep*. David Britland is also the force behind the BBC3 series, *The Real Hustle* that he developed along with Matt Crook and Objective Productions, and is a consultant producer for the hugely popular Derren Brown shows.

In 2005 he was awarded a Literary Fellowship by the Academy of Magical Arts.

Chapter One

I confess I had never seen my friend Holmes so downhearted. He sat in his dressing gown, his grey eyes staring into the distance, his hands clutching that morning's *Times*, which lay closed across his lap. He had been that way since breakfast which still lay untouched on the table, a testament to his dark disposition.

The same brooding frame of mind had occupied him for several days. He seemed inattentive to those who called at his door requesting his assistance, and the previous day had refused to help some poor soul with a rudeness, that was so out of character I had to reprimand him for it. He begged my forgiveness, of course, and that of the client but he made no offer to tell me what troubled him. Today Holmes sank even deeper into whatever abyss had consumed him and hardly seemed aware of my presence in the room. At times like this I usually take a brisk walk believing that a judicious absence may at least lighten my mind if not his, but a heavy fog shrouded London as if Holmes's dismal mood had stretched out beyond the walls of 221B Baker Street and into the surrounding streets. Instead I remained indoors, sitting by the fire, which kept the winter chill at bay. I passed the time by reading old copies of the *British Medical Journal* and compiling notes on one of our more interesting adventures, with a view to having it published in *The Strand* magazine. I had intended to peruse a volume of Poe's mystery stories, which I had purchased in Charing Cross, but in the circumstances I decided that it made for morbid reading and had cast it aside for another less sombre day.

I am no Doctor Freud and was therefore unable to diagnose the cause of my friend's mental affliction. Broken bones not broken minds are my speciality. But I had learned something of Holmes's methods of deduction and it was clear to me that the root of his demeanour lay in the contents of the newspaper that lay folded over his lap. For the past few days he had taken an unusually keen interest in the contents of *The Times*. I was used to his scouring the papers from cover to cover in search of seemingly trivial pieces of data; his masterful brain would stitch them together to form a colourful patchwork of hidden London. Often a tiny remark in a foreign report or a seemingly innocent personal advertisement in the agony column would provide the key to a mystery that had baffled our friends at Scotland Yard. To Holmes the words of a newspaper were a code to be broken and in this he was singularly successful. But recently he had taken to seizing the newspaper and then after a mere glance had thrown it aside as if what he had hoped to find was not there. I had gathered them up and stacked them by his chair where they remained untouched.

On this cold foggy January morning my dear friend had taken *The Times* with his usual rapidity and had barely turned the pages when his gaze became transfixed and he slumped back into his chair. And there I knew he would remain, sitting silently, staring off into the distance thinking thoughts I could not fathom and felt unable to question. He was always an austere soul who rarely communicated his feelings even to me. The solving of puzzles was his great gift, his life, and dominated his every day. Sometimes, when bored or devoid of any intriguing criminal case to entertain his intellect, he would take to cocaine or morphine as a means of distracting himself and avoiding the pit of depression into which he would often fall. As a medical man I had admonished him on several occasions regarding the after effects of such stimulants but he had ignored my warnings and soon I learned to ignore his one weakness. In this case, however, he did not recourse to drugs and, selfishly, I was beginning to wish that he had.

Unable to remain silent any longer while my friend suffered, I walked over to where he sat and snatched the paper from him, saying, "I cannot stand by, Holmes, while some secret grief tears you apart."

He looked up at me as if affronted by my audacity but I fired off another verbal broadside before he could speak.

"Holmes, I apologise for my impudence but is it not equally impudent of you not to share whatever it is that ails you? I am your friend."

I could see that I now had his attention. Before he could respond I raised my finger as a teacher would to a child and continued, knowing full well that if I did not finish now I might not finish at all.

"We have been through many adventures, Holmes, risked our reputations and our lives to save others. Time and again we have taken on the impossible and beaten it. Time and again we have gone where angels and Scotland Yard have feared to tread. And yet now, when I think you need most help, you have shut me out."

There was an awful silence and I thought that I had gone too far. Holmes looked up at me, his eyebrows arched in surprise.

"My dear Watson," said Holmes as he got up from his chair, but before he could say more I put my hand on his shoulder and pushed him down. He looked at me aghast. Knowing I had, for once, the advantage I pressed on.

"No, no more 'dear Watson' until you listen to what I have to say. Holmes, we have shared a great part of our lives together and yet in some respects I know as little about you as the clients who walk through that door. I respect your privacy, of course, but the melancholy brooding that presently consumes you is testing both our energies. Am I not your friend and ally, Holmes? Can we not share this burden and thereby lighten the mood which infects this household?"

His brow furrowed as if bewildered by my outburst. For a moment he regarded me thoughtfully and a flicker of his former self showed itself in his face. Then he spoke.

"I am so embarrassed, my dear Watson. I have been more selfish than you suspect. I have surprised even myself during the last few days but this morning I am perplexed beyond all reason."

Glad that he was at last communicating I tried to untangle the net in which he found himself. "And you have found this perplexing puzzle in *The Times*, I dare say."

"You are right, Watson. I was, as you may have gathered, increasingly anxious about the contents of the newspaper but what I read today has made me feel as if the world is a stranger to me. It makes no sense. And what is worse, neither does my reaction to this dreadful news."

"Then I'm right," I said, "but what on earth could you find in a newspaper that would drive you to such despair?"

"I'm afraid, Watson, you may find the whole affair entirely dishonourable and unworthy of me."

"Then tell me and I will be the judge of what I do or don't find honourable," I said, feeling that I was just a hairsbreadth from understanding the enigma that had confounded me.

Holmes stood up – this time I did not push him down – and took the paper from me. He opened it and spread it across the table and over the breakfast tray.

"There," he said, "that is the cause of my depression and I shan't be at all surprised if you laugh."

I stared down at *The Times*, my eyes passing from one report to the next in an effort to seek out the offender. But I searched in vain. The tribulations detailed there seemed petty and insignificant. A report of the arrangements to be made for the forthcoming visit of some foreign dignitary, a notice of a lecture to be given at the British Museum and an announcement of a new exhibition which was to be opened by Tussaud's. Apart from a collection of advertisements for Borwick's Baking Powder and Nestle's Milk there seemed to be little else. Unwilling to give up my advantage I looked again and, despite Holmes's impatient stare, took time to examine the articles more thoroughly. And though it still was not clear to me I read aloud the piece concerning a Dr. Karl Schermann.

"Dr. Karl Schermann will deliver a lecture on the uses of psycho-graphology in the analysis of ancient texts. Dr. Schermann specialises in the discernment of character from the clues contained within handwriting and has amazed experts from the Manuscripts Department with his character studies of many long dead scribes. Dr. Schermann has been consulted by a number of European police agencies who believe that the technique will provide an invaluable resource in the fight against crime. Dr. Schermann is presently helping Scotland Yard with their investigation into the Mayfair Murders."

"I don't understand Holmes," I said, "What is psycho-graphology?"

"It is nonsense, Watson, that's what it is. Sheer nonsense, and Dr. Schermann is no more than a charlatan. It is an affront to our intelligence that he will sully the halls of the British Museum with his lecture. He will make fools of them all."

He strode across the room, waving his arms in exasperation. "Several days ago when I read in the papers that Schermann had arrived in this country I had hoped he would come and go quickly. I have observed his travels across Europe from Germany and Vienna to France. Two weeks ago the Paris gendarmerie awarded him a medal for his help and then he crossed the Channel to practise his hokum in London. He is a charlatan, Watson, you have my word upon it."

I still did not understand why Holmes should be so furious. He has often thought the police foolish and so could hardly be surprised at what had transpired.

"But, Holmes, I do not see what concern this is of yours?"

"Don't you see, Watson? The article confirms my worst fears. While I am left to deal with humdrum crimes brought to me by servants and tradesmen there is a crime of horrendous magnitude waiting for the right man to solve it."

I knew he was talking about the recent murders in Mayfair and I knew that he thought he was the man to solve them. Holmes had followed the reports with great interest, predicting that Lestrade would come knocking on our door at any moment. But we had heard nothing from Lestrade and the murderer was still at large.

Holmes paced the floor like a man who had just discovered his wife had left him. "And instead of coming to me they have taken up with that buffoon Schermann."

Now it was clear. Holmes was annoyed at Schermann but he was even more annoyed at Lestrade who had not come calling upon our Baker Street lodgings. Yet Holmes, the cool logician and England's finest consulting detective, could not understand why this plagued him so. But I could. The dark force that had possessed Holmes was the one emotion he had in abundance. His vanity.

Chapter Two

Mystery followed Sherlock Holmes like a dark shadow. It was his constant companion and he was never more alive than when it knocked upon his door and made its presence felt, never happier than when there was a problem to be solved or an enigma that required his unique expertise. He thrived on adventure, and I too had been caught up in his zeal and had taken to writing accounts of some of his most noteworthy cases for the popular magazines. And although he frequently admonished me for what he liked to call my 'embellishments', I do believe that Holmes enjoyed the recognition that came with each published tale.

The Metropolitan Police Force was less enthusiastic. Publicly they readily acknowledged the help he gave them. Privately they were often less than grateful. The police were still an object of public suspicion with corruption amongst the constabulary being rife. Dismissals, demotions and resignations were frequent and morale among officers had never been lower. A strike at Bow Street some years ago should have highlighted the terrible pressure and harsh discipline that officers were working under. Instead, it hardened public opinion against them. London quickly forgot the successes of its police force, choosing to remember its failures, while Sherlock Holmes remained celebrated the world over. Even our friend

Inspector Lestrade was affected by the climate of distrust and had avoided our company for some time lest he be thought by his superiors to be consorting with the enemy.

I had noticed that, while Holmes remained as busy as ever with smaller trifles, the cases of note, and I may say, public import had dwindled. I had said nothing to Holmes about the matter, considering it a temporary lull, but in my heart I felt that something was amiss and I laid the blame squarely on our recent adventure at Abbey Grange.

It was a sordid matter, the murder of a brutal man by the lover of his abused wife. It was a rare case too, one in which Holmes and I conspired to act as judge and jury and rather than hand the man over to the police we had decided to set him free. We had our reasons, of course, but I wondered then, and wonder now, whether we acted in haste. It is difficult to keep such a thing secret and Hopkins, the police inspector in charge, was no fool. I have no doubt that if he had not guessed our actions he had at least an inkling that all was not right. Perhaps he told Inspector Lestrade of his suspicions. It would certainly explain the wall of silence that confronted us and the lack of any communication from Scotland Yard over those last few weeks.

Meanwhile the Mayfair murders were the talk of London, mentioned in every household but ours. The grisly title bestowed upon this case was chosen by the press, probably dreamt up in some tavern when time was short and talk was loose. If it was designed to capture the imagination and be memorable, it was a feat it achieved admirably on both counts. That such gruesome slayings could be expressed in words that rolled so easily off the tongue without thought or grief gave me great pause for sadness. I confess that even I gave the killings no particular thought. Three young women – Jane Little, Mary Elizabeth Frank and Susan James – had been murdered in the early weeks of the year – each strangled. Each found dead in Mayfair. The press connected the three events immediately and although I had no reason to doubt them, I also did not envisage that this would be the beginning of a trail of violence that would shake London to its core.

Murder, unfortunately, is commonplace. A man slain in his own home, the doors locked and the windows bolted, was the stuff of which our adventures were made. There at least was mystery. But a murder on the streets at night did not hold the same fascination. I had seen the face of death too many times, both as Holmes's companion and as a soldier in Afghanistan. I had grown blasé, something for which I am now thoroughly ashamed.

If I have any defence it is that I was more worried for my friend Holmes than three victims I had never met. He seemed constantly morose and ill tempered, wishing that every knock at the door was Lestrade seeking his help and sinking ever deeper into depression upon discovering that it was not. Since reading of the arrival of Dr. Schermann, Holmes had not left our lodgings and I resolved to break the deadlock that held us. And so one rare fogless winter morning, his post still unopened on his desk, I persuaded my friend to leave behind all thought of work and join me for lunch. Reluctantly he agreed and at noon we found ourselves sitting at a table at Simpson's dining rooms in the Strand enjoying a delicious meal of roast beef and each other's company. We discussed several of our past cases and which adventures I might consider submitting to *The Strand*. Conspicuous by their absence was any talk of Lestrade, the Mayfair murders or the unfortunate episode at Abbey Grange.

After lunch we left Simpson's only to find ourselves confronted by a fine grey drizzle. Deciding not to walk, Holmes hailed a cab and we set off to Bradley's in search of fresh tobacco. I availed myself of a fine Arcadia while Holmes purchased the strongest leaf to be found in the shop. We departed pleased and felt the rest of the day to be our own. By this time the drizzle had all but vanished and Holmes suggested we peruse the galleries around Bond Street. It was a gentle walk, peering at the many unusual wares on offer, which eventually brought us to Cantle's auction house where a sale of items from the late Lord Dalby's estate was taking place.

"Come," said Holmes, "let us see what aristocratic treasures are to be had." I was taken aback by his enthusiasm for I had never known him to attend an auction before. Dalby had been a notorious gambler and womaniser and stories of his riotous living were the talk of every inn and tavern in London. His name was synonymous with hell raising and the often grotesque stories about him filled those newspapers for whom tittle-tattle was as essential as printers' ink. For his wife it meant shame and humiliation, and unable to endure any more she finally took her own life. She was barely in the grave when Lord Dalby's own body was found drowned in the lake on his estate. And now here we were, like vultures, about to pick over the bones of two ruined lives.

None of these thoughts appeared to trouble my companion and so, carried away by his zeal, I confess that I readily followed him into Cantle's. The business was neither as prestigious as Sotheby's nor as popular as Christie and Manson's but it seemed respectable enough and the clientele, of which there were many, were richly dressed. The auction room was large, lit by two rows of ornate chandeliers that stretched along the high ceiling. There was an air of excitement with much chatter and as we arrived people were already taking their seats in preparation for the sale. We moved through the throng towards a table where I could see a pile of catalogues. "We appear to have alighted upon some important event," I said. "And look, over there, isn't that ..." I turned to Holmes only to discover that he was no longer at my side. Wraithlike he had disappeared. I craned my neck to look over the heads of the crowd but could not see him anywhere. I did, however, see the entrance to the side room where the sale items were on display and pushed my way towards it, apologising profusely to each and every person I bumped into, not that any of them seemed to notice.

The display room was equally crowded and it was some minutes before I found Holmes studying a collection of paintings that hung, temporarily at least, along the furthest wall. They were of remarkable quality though perhaps more a tribute to the late Lord Dalby's wealth than his good taste.

Some of the larger pictures were arranged on easels and Holmes stood before them, his catalogue in hand, and looking every inch the prospective buyer.

"Find anything you like?" I asked.

"Nothing I would hang in Baker Street, but if the crowd is anything to go by there seems to be much of interest." Holmes's eyes scanned the picture in front of him as if somehow he was able to interrogate the artist that painted it. Then, having taken in its details, he moved to the next, a large landscape, and submitted it to an equally intense examination.

"I never knew you were much interested in art, Holmes," I said. He lowered his catalogue and relaxed his steely gaze.

"Why, Watson, I am born of artistic blood. My grandmother was the sister of an artist." It was true. I had forgotten that Holmes was related to the great painter Vernet. "And while I might not create with the paints I am capable of some artistic appreciation. My own art is based upon observation, is it not? These paintings make ideal case studies for any detective."

I wondered what Holmes could possibly mean. How could a painting of pigment and canvas be of use to Holmes? I asked him to explain.

"Watson," he said, "do I detect some scepticism in your voice? Why, this room is a veritable treasure trove of clues. Every picture tells a story, as the old adage says, but perhaps not quite one the artist had intended. Too often the artist puts more of himself into his work than he would like us to know."

"Then what can you tell from the pictures here?"

"A myriad of things, my dear fellow. A stroke of the brush tells me whether an artist is left or right handed, the pressure his strength, and the colour his mood."

"You are surely being simplistic," I ventured.

"Not at all. Who could deny that Van Gogh's work reveals an inner turmoil?"

"But that is an extreme, is it not?"

"I cite it merely as an example that even you can appreciate, Watson. But the evidence is all around you. Why did Corot paint dawn landscapes and Rosa scenes of demonism, while Greuze busied himself with portraits of coy young girls? It is no accident that an artist's disposition is reflected in his work."

I did as Holmes requested and looked closely at the pictures surrounding us. I examined the Rosa that lay on the table, a dark, malevolent picture of a witches' Sabbath, and compared it to the Corot beside it. One artist favoured, or feared, the night while another rose early to capture God's glory on canvas. I thought about what Holmes had said and then turned to reply only to find that he had again left me and had moved to the middle of the room where he was now examining the furniture.

Drawers were opened, hinges tested, cushions felt and table legs scrutinised. He studied the wood with the passion and eye of a master craftsman. "Well?" I asked.

"Surely you can guess, Watson?"

"That each article tells a story?"

"Quite."

"Then what does this writing desk tell you?" I asked indicating the item he had just been examining.

"More than you would think. It's eighteenth century and has a walnut veneer, that much is obvious. It belonged to Lady Dalby and she used it to write her correspondence. The catalogue tells us that much."

He ran his fingers over the top of the desk, and added, "The desk has not been used for many years, having been accidentally damaged at some early point in its history. The marks of restoration are obvious – as too is the cracking of the wood that the changes of temperature would bring as the desk was moved from the cold of storage to the warmth of the house. It did however see better times, being positioned against a window, so that the writer could benefit from the light. You can clearly see how the sun has bleached the wood. And yet, despite its newfound position, Lady Dalby chose to write her correspondence in the dark of the evening. Very strange, I think you would agree. But then she was a very secretive woman. Compassionate too.

"I grant you that the state of the wood might tell you something of the article's history, but how do you arrive at the conclusion that she wrote by night?"

"Simple," said Holmes, "the desktop is stained in several places by candle wax and the wood not properly cleaned."

"Ah, and the fact that she wrote by candlelight suggests that she may have had something to hide."

"On the contrary. Candle wax may indicate nothing more than lack of any other type of illumination."

"Then why do you think Lady Dalby was secretive?"

"Because of this," said Holmes, whereupon he opened the drawer of the desk once more and then gave the handle a sharp twist to the left. To my astonishment a flap of wood sprang open to reveal a secret compartment.

"Whatever Lady Dalby was writing she certainly didn't want it found. I believe she hid the correspondence here until it could be delivered. It is pure speculation but I wonder what part this desk played in the Dalby tragedy."

"I don't follow you, Holmes."

"Secret correspondence generally suggests one of two things, spying or blackmail. I would never have taken Lady Dalby for a spy. But as I say, it is sheer speculation and not something I have been asked to enquire into."

Suddenly possibilities suggested themselves that would lead to a better understanding of the events on the Dalby estate. Was Lady Dalby being blackmailed? About what ... her husband? Is that what caused their deaths? Holmes's razor sharp mind had cut through the mystery and found a light at its core. I wondered how he had managed to detect what others had failed to see.

"How did you know about the secret compartment?"

"The drawer was made relatively recently. Note the machined joints holding the panels in place. The rest of the desk is handmade, as it should be. A woman keen to conceal her activities might also be keen to hide whatever it was that she was writing. A hidden compartment is a common solution to such a problem."

Holmes clicked the flap shut and closed the drawer as if that was an end to the matter.

"Oh, and you said she was compassionate. What evidence did you find for that?"

"Cat scratches, Watson."

"Pardon?"

"Cat scratches. They are all over the lower panels of the desk. Only a woman who loved her cat more than her furniture would have allowed such obvious vandalism to go on."

For most people present the auction provided an opportunity for easy profit. For Holmes it was a gallery of the mind, a repository of clues and insights and hints of stories yet to be told.

We were about to leave the room and take our seats for the auction when a figure suddenly stepped back from the crowd and trod squarely on my foot. The pain was excruciating and I gave out a loud cry that brought the chattering room to silence. I turned around to berate my assailant and came face to face with one of the prettiest young ladies it has ever been my good fortune to meet.

"I'm very sorry," she said. "Please accept my apologies." I ignored my throbbing foot and was captivated by two magnificent blue eyes coquettishly staring in my direction and a smile that banished all thoughts of pain. What a remarkable creature she was. Small – petite, one might say – dressed in a blue silk brocade and with a pale face framed by blonde tresses and fashionable curls. But it was her eyes that transfixed me and rendered me speechless. It was as if the comely subject of Greuze's painting had stepped gently down from the wall.

"Don't worry about it," said Holmes breaking whatever spell held me. "He's a doctor; I'm sure he can mend a broken foot, especially his own."

"Yes, I'm a doctor," said I, still searching for something more sensible to say.

"Well, I am truly sorry," she replied smiling and then turned to join the man next to her who was examining some jewellery.

I said farewell but it went unheard and Holmes and I took our seats at the back of the auction room. We had no sooner sat down than my pain returned. Holmes noticed me wincing as I stroked my poor foot.

"I take it she was heavier than she looked," he said and added with not a little laughter, "Physician heal thyself." Then a bell rang to indicate that the auction was about to begin.

"Do you really want to stay for the sale, Holmes, or should we move on?"

"Oh we'll certainly stay," Holmes said, "At least until you can walk again."

"That's very kind of you, Holmes."

"Not at all. Besides, I think there is much to interest us here, your accident notwithstanding." He opened his catalogue and began to read, "And you never know, you might bump into your young lady again."

It was then that I remembered whom I had seen earlier in the crowd.

"I almost forgot to tell you," I said. "There is another secret admirer of the arts here besides yourself."

"And who would that be, Watson?"

"Why, he's over there," I said, nodding my head in our visitor's direction. Holmes looked up, and for once, the surprise was evident on his face.

"Well, well," he whispered, "what on earth brings our friend here? I warrant it is not because of his fondness for painting."

Our acquaintance seemed peculiarly absorbed in his catalogue and unwilling to meet our gaze.

"Do you think he is trying to ignore us?" I asked.

"I'm certain of it," whispered Holmes. "If he is here, then trouble is afoot, if you'll pardon the expression. Let us play the game quietly until the rules are revealed."

It was clear that some crime was about to invade this fine establishment and I marvelled at the way Holmes had been drawn here like iron to a lodestone. The seats gradually filled with people as the last of them filed from the display room and took their places. Then the auctioneer banged his hammer and announced that the sale had begun. The first item, a portrait by Greuze, was introduced and a bid was quickly made. Holmes consulted his catalogue and I cast a curious glance over at our friend and wondered what mystery had brought Inspector Lestrade to Cantle's.

Chapter Three

The auctioneer was a tall, lean fellow who looked to be in need of one of Mrs. Hudson's suppers. He had high cheekbones and a pale face out of which shone two stony dark eyes, and he waved his hands around excitedly like a marionette when he talked, and banged a hammer on top of the podium at which he stood whenever a sale was made. Half an hour had passed and the event had gone well. The Greuze, a portrait of a peasant girl, which, as Holmes had noted, had an coy quality about it, was sold for a sum that matched the catalogue estimate. I recalled that Greuze was a favourite of Moriarty's. I could see why.

Following that was a parade of vivid landscapes interspersed with some sombre portraits so dark that I could barely make them out from my seat at the back of the hall. Holmes was paying close attention to everything that happened and he did not turn to look at Lestrade once. I, on the other hand, did casually glance in his direction from time to time, usually when a bid was made from that part of the room. It seemed to me that Lestrade wasn't paying the slightest bit of attention to the sale. He appeared to be merely waiting, but waiting for what I did not know. On one occasion our eyes met and he quickly looked elsewhere, as did I for fear I might give the game away, whatever the game was.

Eventually my attention began to wane. The sale grew less interesting the longer it continued and I turned to Holmes for some indication as to how long we would remain here.

"Exciting, is it not?" said Holmes, the first time he had spoken to me since the auction began.

"I suppose so," I answered not wishing to spoil my friend's enjoyment. Anything was better than sitting in Baker Street watching him fret.

"There's no supposing about it. Look at them bidding, see the fever in their eyes when they win their prize, and the disappointment when they lose. I dare say it harks back to some primeval instinct."

"Akin to hunting?"

"The very same. Instead of spears and sticks they use money to bring their prey down."

I realised that Holmes too wasn't the slightest bit concerned with the articles on sale, finding the buyers infinitely more interesting. I took to watching them to occupy my time, noting their dress, manner, age, accents and a list of other minute details in an attempt to apply Holmes's analytical techniques and draw up a portrait of my own. I learned quickly that all was not clear. The ostentatiously rich bid often, as would be expected, but then so did several gentlemen who were far less well attired, indeed some of them presented quite a shabby appearance. Possibly they were buying on behalf of another. Perhaps they were dealers themselves. The truth was that I did not know. I longed to ask Holmes his opinion but he was far too busy watching the auction.

I soon grew weary and was verging on sleep when Holmes brushed against me as his arm shot up into the air. "One hundred pounds," said the auctioneer and pointed in our direction. For a moment I thought he had been pointing at me and that I had accidentally nodded while dozing. Then I saw Holmes's arm raised and knew that he was the bidder. It was the turn of the furniture to be sold and I saw that the walnut desk was now on display.

As the bidding continued I leaned across to Holmes and asked him where the item was listed in the catalogue. He pointed to a desk listed on the page and then raised his hand again. "One hundred and ten pounds," said the auctioneer. The price was high and I could not see what had stimulated Holmes's interest in what I thought to be a rather dull piece. The estimate in the catalogue was only £70. I tried to point this out to Holmes but he ignored me and shot up his hand once more. "One hundred and twenty pounds," said the auctioneer. "One hundred and twenty pounds I am bid. Any more takers? Going at one hundred and twenty pounds. Going ... going ..."

"Have you taken leave of your senses, Holmes? It's hardly worth that."

"Art is worth what you pay for it, my dear Watson. And it seems that I am not the only one interested in this item."

The auctioneer was about to bring down his hammer when someone in the front row raised their hand and made another bid. "One hundred and twenty-five pounds at the front, sir. Any more?" The auctioneer looked at Holmes and for a second I thought that he was going to continue his bidding. Instead he shook his head and the hammer was brought down on the sale.

"What was all that about?" I asked.

"Just an experiment," replied Holmes.

"Yes but what would have happened if you had won?"

"Then my experiment would have been a failure, my lodgings more crowded and my pocket a tad lighter. But as you saw it has been a success."

I was about to point out that he had lost the desk not won it but instead said, "Then I congratulate you on your experiment but perhaps it is time to go."

"Dear me, no. The drama has hardly begun."

"And what drama is that," I enquired.

"Frankly, Watson, I have no idea, that is why I intend to stay and find out. How is our friend Lestrade?" I looked over in his direction. He was staring straight at me and this time was unable or unwilling to shake my gaze.

"He seems much more interested in our presence now," I said.

"I thought so, but it will soon wear off. He'll make a note in his book and then carry on as if he has never seen us." Holmes was right. Lestrade reached into his pocket, removed a small notebook and jotted something down on its pages. He then resumed his nonchalant supervision of the room.

"Ah, here is the next lot," said Holmes, with enthusiasm, and with that he ceased all conversation and concentrated his mind on the auction, leaving me to wonder what other surprises the afternoon might bring.

Chapter Four

The two hours had passed before a break was called. Holmes had made no more bids and Lestrade paid us no more attention. Once again we made our way to the display room where nearly two thirds of the items where now marked with labels indicating that they had been sold. Most of what remained was jewellery that had once belonged to the unfortunate Lady Dalby. It was arranged in a large glittering display across two large counters and was clearly of far greater value than any of the furniture. Several people were asking for a closer look at the items and auction staff handed them over for appraisal. The young lady I had met earlier was there with her male companion. He was wearing a loupe and examining an ostentatious diamond ring. She saw me approach and gave a distinctly flirtatious smile.

"How's your foot?" she asked.

"Much better," I said.

And then I heard a familiar voice behind me, "And how is your desk?" It was Holmes. At first I had no idea what he meant but all was made clear when the young lady spoke.

"Oh, you must be the gentleman I was bidding against."

"Yes," said Holmes, "I was sorry to lose it but I'm sure it will fare better in your home than mine. By the way, let me introduce myself, my name is Sherlock Holmes and this is Dr. Watson."

I swear the bloom faded from her cheeks when she heard our names. And her companion, whom I had thought to be wholly involved with his examination of the diamond, let the loupe drop from his eye and turned towards us in an instant.

"Sherlock Holmes and Doctor Watson! Why, who could have guessed that we would meet two such famous men here today?" he said.

He was in his early thirties, smartly dressed, with dark hair and a thin waxed moustache of the type favoured by Europeans. He extended a hand towards Holmes and introduced himself.

"I am Archibald Sancy and this is my fiancée Miss Emily Hope. We're very pleased to meet you. I've read much of your exploits."

"Some of them are even true," said Holmes smiling.

Mr. Sancy was about to say more when one of Cantle's staff tapped him on the shoulder. Sancy turned, suddenly realised what the problem was and then handed back the diamond ring he had been holding.

"We won't detain you any longer," said Holmes, "I can see that you and Miss Hope are busy."

"Perhaps we'll see each other later," said Sancy.

"Perhaps," said Holmes. He wandered back into the auction room and I quickly said my goodbyes and followed him.

It wasn't until we were once more in our seats that I spoke.

"Well, call me suspicious, Holmes, but I thought our little exchange there was most odd."

"Indeed it was, Watson. Miss Hope has been flirting with you outrageously and ..."

"Oh I wouldn't say that," I interrupted.

"Outrageously," repeated Holmes, "while all along she is engaged to be married to Mr. Sancy."

I felt my face warm with embarrassment.

"I don't know whether to feel sorry for Mr. Sancy or give my sympathy to Miss Hope. She flirts and he allows it. Does that not seem strange to you, Watson?"

I said nothing.

"And what is worse," said Holmes, clearly enjoying himself, "is that he has the audacity to lie to us."

"Lie, about what?"

"About everything. Clearly they are not engaged, Watson, and I find it very unlikely that their names are Hope and Sancy."

"And why is that?"

"Because they are the names of two of the world's largest diamonds. Perhaps the young gentleman's imagination was inspired by the jewellery he was inspecting. My guess is that our young couple are the very people that Lestrade is watching."

"But why? What could they have done?"

"I believe, Watson, that they are jewel thieves. Or more specifically he is the thief and she his accomplice."

Holmes did not make such accusations lightly and I knew that we would be at Cantle's until the final act of the drama had been played out. Hope and Sancy, or whatever their real names might be, were under surveillance by Inspector Lestrade, while Lestrade himself was under Holmes's watchful eye. I did not think this would endear us to the good Inspector but Holmes was far more interested in the case than any personal repercussions it may have. For myself, I kept silent, already feeling foolish at having been so easily distracted by a pretty face, and tried to keep from dozing as the auctioneer's mournful tones droned on.

Chapter Five

A sharp piercing screech brought me to attention. I looked over to the side of the room and saw Lestrade blowing hard on his police whistle. He blew again and this time another whistle sounded in response. It came from behind me and I turned and saw that four constables had entered the auction room and were now barring the door. Several other men stood up from among the seated bidders and took positions at all the entrances and exits around the room. I presumed that they too were policemen, dressed in street clothes so that they could blend in with the crowd.

"What happened, Holmes?" I asked.

"One of the staff whispered something into Lestrade's ear and that prompted him into action. If I'm not mistaken the moment Lestrade has been waiting for has finally arrived."

The room had become extremely agitated and boisterous as people asked why the auction had been halted in such an abrupt and disruptive fashion. One man tried to leave the building and berated the constables when he was pushed back. Another shouted out, demanding an explanation from Lestrade. The staff of Cantle's were huddled together discussing the situation with the auctioneer who, upon being appraised of the problem, then banged his hammer on the podium several times to gain attention. The room quietened and he began to speak.

"Gentlemen, ladies, I'm afraid I have a serious announcement to make. As you will see the building has been surrounded by the Metropolitan Police. I would appreciate your cooperation. You need do nothing but sit quietly until their investigation is over."

"What investigation?" cried a man in the front row.

"It is a matter of theft," said the auctioneer. He looked over to Lestrade as if to gain his permission before saying any more. Lestrade nodded and the auctioneer continued.

"A quantity of jewellery has been stolen. The police, led by Inspector Lestrade, will now commence an enquiry. I understand that the thief has been under surveillance for some time and that the matter can be concluded quickly, after which the auction will continue. But for now, it will expedite matters if you would all remain in your seats."

The crowd did not take this news with good grace and there were many murmurs of disapproval. They took no pains to disguise their annoyance at being held captive even if their imprisonment was to be short. They resented their time being stolen along with the jewellery.

"Come, Watson, let us see if we can be of service," said Holmes.

As we left our seats a constable asked us to return but upon hearing our names allowed us to pass. When we reached Lestrade he was deep in conversation and when he finally spoke to us it was not without a hint of bitterness.

"Please, Holmes, I am in the middle of an enquiry. If you wish to leave now I will have one of my men accompany you to the door. If you do not wish to leave I would rather you sat down and waited until the matter is concluded."

"Perhaps I can help you conclude the matter more swiftly," answered Holmes.

"I think not, Mr. Holmes. We wish to apprehend the suspects not set them free," said Lestrade, making a veiled reference to the incident at Abbey Grange and confirming my worst suspicions. "Please leave me to do my duty."

Lestrade would happily have let us leave but the gentleman he had been talking to was not prepared to turn away help so easily. He extended a hand and introduced himself.

"My name is Edmund Cantle, proprietor of this establishment. I take it you are Mr. Sherlock Holmes?"

"That I am," said Holmes, "and this is my esteemed friend and colleague Dr. Watson."

We shook hands, Lestrade clearly embarrassed by our presence as Edmund Cantle explained the facts of the case.

"As you may have gathered, Mr. Holmes, a substantial quantity of jewellery has gone missing. At some time during the auction it has been exchanged for paste replicas. Come, let me show you."

Mr. Cantle led us to the display cases where a member of his staff was examining the contents. Several items were arranged on the counter.

"Do you have an inventory of what is missing?" asked Mr. Cantle.

"All these are fake," said the gentleman behind the counter. "The real items are all missing ... stolen."

Lestrade pushed his way forward. "There is nothing to worry about, Mr. Cantle. We knew this would happen, we have the suspects in custody and now it is merely a matter of recovering the jewellery."

"How did you know the theft was to take place?" I said.

"We arrested the man who produced the fakes on an entirely different matter. He was glad to inform upon his clients in the hope of leniency."

Holmes examined the paste jewellery while Edmund Cantle peered over his shoulder.

"And what do you estimate the value of the genuine items to be?" asked Holmes.

"Thousands, simply thousands," replied Cantle.

"Fortunately," said Lestrade, "we knew the thief's plan in advance and that he would be here today using the name of Archibald Sancy. His real name is Stanley Higson, an adroit sleight of hand artist whose modus operandi is to switch the real jewellery for fakes as he examines them. He looks a little different from the photographs we have at the station. The moustache is a new acquisition as is the girl, Miss Hope."

"I think you'll find that is a pseudonym too," said Holmes.

"No matter. We'll soon get to the bottom of it. They are being searched even as I speak.

A constable joined us and addressed Lestrade.

"We have searched the suspects sir but they do not have the jewellery."

"Excuse me, gentlemen, it seems that I am required." He accompanied the constable to an office at the far end of the display room. As the door opened I saw Miss Hope sitting at a table inside. I think she smiled at me. Then the door closed and I could hear Lestrade's voice from within, loud and angry.

Edmund Cantle turned to Holmes and asked if there was anything that could be done.

"We had better wait until the Inspector has completed his interrogation," said Holmes. "He's a thorough man but perhaps not in the clearest of minds at the moment. But I wouldn't worry about the stolen items. It is only a matter of time before they are recovered.

Some time passed before Lestrade emerged from the office, clearly no wiser than when he entered.

"They have disposed of the stolen items," said Lestrade, somewhat exasperated.

"Then you do not have a case, Inspector," said Holmes.

"I don't know what you mean. We caught them red-handed."

"I think not. Consider the facts. The jewellery is missing and paste articles are found in their place."

"Yes, the very articles that Higson had made by a man we have in custody."

"I'm afraid that the word of a convicted felon would count for very little in a court of law. The man you have would say anything to lessen his sentence, would he not?"

Lestrade had to admit that such a thought had crossed his mind.

"Did anyone see Higson switch the jewellery?" asked Holmes.

"No. The man is an accomplished thief. You wouldn't see the switch even if he did it right under your nose. You know that, Holmes."

"Indeed I do. So there are no witnesses, no jewellery and only the word of a criminal bargaining for his freedom. And Miss Hope – do you have anything against her?"

"Not yet, but what would she be doing with such a man if she ..." Lestrade's words grew mumbled as he realised that Holmes was right. There was not a shred of evidence against the pair.

"I do not care who the suspects are, Inspector Lestrade, or what happens to them after today, I merely wish the recovery of the items. You must begin a search of the entire building at once," said Cantle.

"There may be some difficulty there, as the good Inspector knows," said Holmes.

"That is true," said Lestrade. "We have already searched many of the rooms, including this one, but any one of the people in this building could have the jewellery on their person. We cannot search them all and we cannot hold them much longer against their will."

"Then what is to be done?" asked Mr. Cantle.

Lestrade considered the matter carefully but the dilemma proved too much for him. Disturbing Cantle's illustrious clientele was not something to be taken lightly. Holmes was waiting patiently, expecting Lestrade to give up his pride and ask for help but before he could, Edmund Cantle spoke.

"Mr. Holmes, you said earlier that you might be of assistance. Is that offer still open?"

"Always," said Holmes.

"Then I shall be glad to take it. Do you think you can find the jewellery without making more trouble than we already have?"

"I will most assuredly try."

"Inspector Lestrade, do we have your help in the matter? I am sure that Mr. Holmes might want to avail himself of whatever support your constables can provide."

Lestrade did not respond immediately but I could see that he found himself trapped between his lack of a better plan and his reluctance to be seen working with Holmes. As it happened a decision was not required for Holmes made the first and most surprising move.

"That will not be necessary, Mr. Cantle. It will take only one man to recover the stolen items."

"And who would that be?" asked Lestrade disdainfully.

"Why my friend, Dr. Watson, of course!"

I was not startled at the mention of my name but Lestrade certainly was. Holmes had played the game well. He was not going to give Lestrade even the satisfaction of claiming he had been bested by the world's greatest consulting detective. He was about to hand that duty to me and it was one I gladly accepted.

"Watson," said Holmes, "you have been with me since we entered this fine establishment and witnessed everything that I have seen. Where would you expect our jewel thieves to have hidden their ill-gotten trove?"

I knew at once what Holmes meant, indeed I had my suspicions all along. Why else would Miss Hope have bid far more than the true value for Lady Dalby's writing desk? I walked over to the desk, Lestrade, Cantle and Holmes following in my wake. I opened the drawer. It was empty.

"We have already searched the desk, Dr. Watson," said Lestrade with some scorn.

I gave the handle a twist just as I had seen Holmes do and the secret compartment suddenly sprang open revealing a hoard of scintillating jewels. Lestrade was beside himself with shock, realising that having already mentioned the failed search he had dug his hole even deeper. Edmund Cantle was ecstatic with relief and patted me on the back in congratulations. Holmes smiled at a job well done.

"I hope we didn't take too long, Mr. Cantle. My friend Watson doesn't have the resources that the Metropolitan Police do. Nevertheless we try to please."

Lestrade's saw that he had been made a fool of but knew he had nobody to blame but himself. It was possible that Holmes and I would remain scapegoats for his failure and that the animosity that had developed between us would remain for some time. But it was also a rare moment of triumph and one to be savoured. Cantle shook our hands and confessed that he had always been a little sceptical of my stories in *The Strand* but now that he had seen the results for himself, we may count him among our greatest admirers. He then left to tell the clients that the jewellery had been found and that the auction would recommence tomorrow. Lestrade offered his congratulations though how well meant they were was difficult to tell. Then he asked Holmes and me if we would be good enough to accompany him to the office and meet his prisoners. We readily agreed.

As we entered the office Miss Hope gave me the same winsome smile that she dispensed so easily while Stanley Higson stood politely and welcomed us as if greeting old friends.

"Mr. Holmes and Dr. Watson. How nice to meet you again."

Lestrade was in no mood for jokes and told him to sit down which he did. He had more pressing matters to discuss. "Mr. Holmes, Dr. Watson, I have a quandary that requires your advice."

"We are always at your service. It is a pity that you do not contact us on a more regular basis," said Holmes.

Lestrade knew well what Holmes was referring to but carried on regardless. "I'll be frank. As a member of the Metropolitan Police Force I would be happy to put these two behind bars for many years."

Higson stroked his moustache and feigned indifference while Miss Hope continued to wear her girlish smile. They were unmoved by their situation and behaved as if it was someone else's fate being discussed rather than their own. Lestrade continued to outline his problem.

"Higson is very well known to the police in several counties. He has been convicted on a variety of matters and is no stranger to Her Majesty's prisons. Miss Hope has yet to be identified. But bearing in mind your earlier advice Mr. Holmes, I am uncertain as to whether there is a case to answer here. The method of the crime has been deduced and the jewellery recovered."

At the mention of this the smile on Miss Hope's lips faded and Higson ceased his preening. The news that the jewels were no longer in their possession was a surprise to both of them. Lestrade noticed the change in their demeanour and addressed his next remarks directly to them. "Yes, I am pleased to say that your actions have come to nought, thanks to my friends Mr. Holmes and Dr. Watson."

I was pleased that he called us his friends and glad that his mood against us had mellowed.

"I'll admit, Holmes, that apart from some highly suspicious circumstantial evidence I have nothing substantial on which to build a case against these rascals. While I have no objection to them spending time in custody, I have, as you must have surmised, better things to be spending my time on if the court case will not deliver a guilty verdict."

"Then what do you propose to do?" asked Holmes, "Let the guilty go free?"

"I fear I have no choice. I just want to be sure I am doing the right thing. I thought that you and Watson having been in a similar situation, you might have some advice to offer."

Holmes thought for a moment and then delivered his verdict. "I take it the more pressing matter is the Mayfair murders and with that I agree. Murder is a darker deed than theft. I also agree that it would be unjust if these two remained unpunished. While they may have been singularly unsuccessful on this occasion, there is no reason to suppose they will choose any other way of life when they leave here. It occurs to me, however, that we have an opportunity to investigate more than the planned theft of jewellery. It is said that a criminal often returns to the scene of a crime. I think that is what has happened here."

Higson stood up immediately and began to protest. "Inspector Lestrade, I must warn you that if you do not release me immediately I will be forced to consider legal action against you and your Force."

"Hey," shouted Miss Hope, her smile long since turned to a grimace, and her pleasant demeanour replaced by a scullery maid's manners, "don't forget about me. I want out of here too."

"Yes, I know, we will both be out soon, my dear, but please let me do the talking."

Holmes raised a finger, which immediately silenced their bickering. "Don't interrupt. It is discourteous. Now where was I? Oh yes, I mentioned that criminals have a habit of returning to the scene of a crime. Have you not wondered how Higson managed to get such accurate reproductions of Lady Dalby's jewellery manufactured? Let us suppose that he has had an opportunity to see them before. Might that be an explanation?"

Higson's eyes betrayed a man whose secret was about to be uncovered. Miss Hope's hand strayed over to his and gripped it tightly, like a child about to be punished.

"And what of the secret compartment in the writing desk. Such things are not easily found. Did they stumble upon it while they were here today or did they have some previous knowledge of its existence? I don't mean to be rude, Miss Hope, but your fine clothes and gentle smile do not conceal the parlour maid's hands which you possess."

She quickly pulled her hand away from Higson's.

"I wonder," said Holmes, "where you might have been previously employed. At Lord and Lady Dalby's estate perhaps? If I were you, Lestrade, I would hold onto these two. They know far more than they have said and I believe they may well be implicated in the deaths that brought this very auction into existence. My guess is that blackmail is at the heart of the matter. Why else would a woman of Lady Dalby's standing throw herself in the lake? Higson found some way to dishonour her and she, unable to take anymore, took the only way out she knew and committed suicide. Her loyal but misguided husband followed suit. My instincts tell me that Higson was the blackmailer and Miss Hope his willing accomplice. I dare say that the blackmail letters were hidden in the secret compartment of Lady Dalby's writing desk and that Miss Hope retrieved them when the situation became dangerous. Beyond that I cannot say, other than to advise that an investigation thoroughly carried out may well prove productive and provide the desired result, a lengthy sentence at Her Majesty's pleasure.

This I had not foreseen but Holmes's incredible suppositions had enough substance to form an investigation, if not a case. I could see that Lestrade agreed. He called for two of his constables. Higson and Hope were handcuffed and led away, protesting their innocence as they went.

"Your help is much appreciated, Mr. Holmes, and yours Dr. Watson. I will let you know how the investigation proceeds."

"It won't be easy," said Holmes, "I suggest you begin with a search of their abode. Criminals are careless, the incriminating is as invisible to their eyes as the harm and misery they create."

"I'll be sure to do a thorough job," said Lestrade. "And I know where to come if I need more help."

We shook hands as if to say goodbye but in a strange way I had the impression that we were really saying hello after a long absence. I expected it would not be long before Lestrade came knocking on our door, anxious to discuss the Mayfair murders. Holmes thought so too. How wrong we were.

Chapter Six

By the next morning the rain that had swept London had cleared. Holmes, never an early riser, awoke around eleven and for the first time in many days ate breakfast and took coffee. I had already been through the newspapers and therefore knew what lay in store for him: another grisly murder, a young woman who had yet to be identified.

This was the fourth murder in as many weeks and the newspapers were already comparing it to those carried out by 'Jack the Ripper'. Many thought the 'Ripper' had returned. Rumours were rife and the letters column of *The Times* quickly filled with ill-informed guesswork. If it was the 'Ripper' why had he come back? Where had be been these last years? Idle gossip generated sensational headlines and column upon column of hearsay, nonsense and speculation. Editorials held the police responsible. They had failed the public in 1888 and they were failing them now.

Dusty notebooks were exhumed and journalists retold their favourite 'Ripper' stories. 'How I nearly caught the Ripper,' boasted one, describing his evening spent with a group of vigilantes in Whitechapel. 'I Was The Ripper,' teased the novelist George R. Sims as he repeated for at least the sixth time the story of the night he was mistaken for the notorious murderer and arrested by the police.

Mr. Sims fancied himself as an expert on the 'Ripper' and put forth many fanciful ideas as to his identity, claiming that he had been told that the police knew perfectly well who the 'Ripper' was and that he had drowned himself in the Thames as an act of remorse. Quite why the police would confide in Mr. Sims was never explained.

Only Sherlock Holmes had remained publicly silent on the matter, his opinion unsought. In private, though, I knew he was busy collating every detail and subjecting it to his rigorous and expert analysis. He did not conjecture or guess or make idle claims. He merely absorbed all that was available, mulling the information over like some great Babbage machine. He had refused to talk even to me about it, pretending that some other more trivial case required his attention before he could consider the facts in London's latest horror. I knew then that he was awaiting Lestrade's call, a call that never came but which was surely imminent following our encounter at Cantle's auction rooms.

Stories about the wonderful Dr. Schermann appeared alongside the details of the murder and recounted with self-proclaimed hyperbole how he had helped solve similar crimes in many European cities. I suspect it was this, the praising of a rival detective that catapulted Holmes into action and made him take a more active role in the case. That morning he seemed alive with fresh possibilities, sorting through his papers and clippings and organising the data necessary to tackle the problem he had set himself. Holmes would solve this mystery, not for Lestrade or London or the four victims and their families, but for himself. And his search for clues would start at the British Museum.

The advertisement in *The Times* had said that Dr Schermann's lecture was to begin at 2.30 p.m. but, as was Holmes's habit, we arrived early, the better to observe our quarry. Chairs had been arranged in the main gallery for some two hundred people and we were amazed to find that some had arrived even earlier than we. At the front of the hall coats were already draped over chairs and programmes placed on seats, an unwritten warning that these prime spots were reserved for their owners. Museum staff were positioning a lectern and we could see that a lantern and screen were already in place together with a box of glass slides. As I was looking around the room, trying to find a familiar face, Holmes nudged my arm.

"There's our man, Watson," said Holmes, as if he had spotted the Mayfair murderer himself.

"That's Dr. Karl Schermann, Scotland Yard's latest addition to the constabulary. A little short don't you think?"

"Really, Holmes," I said, "Your sarcasm is unwarranted. Let us meet the man before we make our opinion of him."

"I was just trying to save time, Watson. No matter."

I had seen Holmes smile and laugh many a time upon solving a case but this was unprecedented. His wit may have been premature but I cannot deny that it added a certain sparkle to the proceedings and had I not been among such eminent company I would have laughed at his remarks. Dr Schermann was indeed short of stature. He seemed highly animated with a wiry frame topped by a noble head. His hair was curly and grey and he looked to be in his fifties. A grey moustache gave him authority and was met on either side of his head by bushy sideburns. His European mannerisms made him appear exceedingly theatrical for a scientist. His hands moved quickly but gracefully as he talked while his dark sparkling eyes danced beneath thin-framed spectacles.

He was accompanied by an elegantly dressed woman of middle years who seemed to hang on his every word.

"It that his wife?" I asked Holmes.

"Not his," said Holmes, "that is Lady Bradford, the wife of the Commissioner of the Metropolitan Police, Sir Edward Bradford. It seems he has friends in high places."

She introduced him to Henry Bloom, the museum's director, and several other dignitaries who were present. Holmes nudged me with his elbow and directed my attention to the other side of the room.

"Look, here comes Lestrade. Quick, let us take our seats at the rear of the hall. I do not want to be seen quite yet."

41

And with that we took our places and waited for the lecture to begin.

Henry Bloom introduced Lestrade, and in turn Lestrade introduced Dr. Schermann to the audience, telling us that the doctor had developed some of the most remarkable forensic techniques he had ever witnessed, at which point I heard my friend Holmes gave out a snort of disapproval.

Dr. Schermann was quite a charmer. The lights went down and, accompanied by a selection of slides, the doctor told us of the many crimes he had been made acquainted with through the offices of several police forces on the Continent. He praised the work of Monsieur Alphonse Bertillon, whom, he had met while in France. Bertillon had devised a method of identifying criminals by means of a system of bodily measurements including colour of eyes, exact length of limbs and the presence of scars and other deformities. It would now take more than a change of name and clothes for a criminal to evade the legal process. Schermann also said he had great hopes for the uses of fingerprinting, which he had observed in India and which promised to provide an even more exact method of identifying the escaped criminal. It was even possible to take prints at the scene of a crime and match them to the hands of the perpetrator. None of this was new to Holmes, who had already talked with Sir Edward Richard Henry about establishing a department dedicated to the use of this technique at Scotland Yard. For a while it looked as if nothing would surprise us. Then a picture of Cesare Lombroso came onto the screen.

"I hope he's not about to sing Lombroso's praises," whispered Holmes. Lombroso was a bright man in many respects but his theory that criminals can be distinguished by physical hereditary traits had long been disproved.

"Perhaps he thinks we should arrest all those with wide noses and long earlobes," I joked.

"No, just those with wiry grey hair and handlebar moustaches," said Holmes, referring to Dr. Schermann himself.

"It is easy to make a mistake," said Dr. Schermann. "Lombroso was a brilliant man. Brilliant. He believed that criminal behaviour is innate. That it exists within the criminal himself and can be passed down from father to son as a disease can be passed from one patient to another."

The audience started to murmur, fearing that Dr. Schermann was about to resurrect Lombroso's scientific folly. Dr. Schermann raised his hands in the air and then gently lowered them as if to calm the audience, which he did.

"No, gentlemen, Lombroso was wrong. He believed criminality can be read in the face of the criminal. It cannot." The audience breathed a sigh of relief and Dr. Schermann, sensing he had them enthralled, quickly said, "But it can be read in his mind. Mr. Bloom could we have the lights please? I think it is time for a demonstration." And with that Lombroso's picture faded from view on the screen as the hall lights revealed that Inspector Lestrade was now standing on stage with another gentleman next to him.

"I do believe that's Richard Spring," said Holmes. "Rather a long way from his prison cell, I think."

Spring was a notorious criminal, a forger of classical paintings whose work had found its way into many galleries and museums and caused no end of embarrassment among the art world's cognescenti. A closer look showed that his left wrist was handcuffed to Lestrade's right. Dr. Schermann introduced Spring to the audience who roared with laughter when Lestrade held up his left arm to reveal the cuffs. Then Dr. Schermann requested the assistance of three volunteers.

"I feel like your Mr. Maskelyne," he said, referring to the popular conjuror who played at the Egyptian Hall, and this drew more laughter from the crowd.

Each of the volunteers and Richard Spring were asked to write something on a slip of paper. "But please, this is a test for me, for my theory. Please make it something that wouldn't identify you. Not even to your closest friend. It can be a line of poetry, the name of an animal, an object in this room. Anything. Anything you think I could not anticipate." And

43

with that he turned his back so that he could not see what was written.

When the writing was done the papers were folded and dropped into a gentleman's hat, which was handed to Inspector Lestrade. Lestrade then passed the hat to the hapless looking Richard Spring.

"I wonder what Spring has done to deserve this humiliation," laughed Holmes. "Bad enough to be in prison but I thought the days of being jeered in public were long gone."

Dr. Schermann, though, basked in the laughter and then raised his arms once again, which immediately quietened the gathering. He asked Inspector Lestrade to reach inside the hat and pull out one of the folded papers. Dr. Schermann unfolded it and as his eyes scanned the text he spoke.

"For over two thousand years we have known that our signatures can reveal something of our character. A hasty note is very different from that made with care. An educated hand differs from that of the ignorant. But we can go further. Aristotle said that men's characters can be divined from their writing. Julius Caesar knew this also and used the technique on many occasions to identify the hands of those who were against him. And in 1622 Professor Camillo Baldo of Bologna made the first academic study of handwriting and the science of graphology was born. Today I offer you a much more refined system which I call psycho-graphology. The study of the mind through handwriting." He walked to the lectern holding the piece of paper high as if it were of great importance. Then, in a flurry of words he started to describe someone.

"The author of this piece is a fine penman indicating a neat and tidy personality. He likes things to be 'in their place.' The writing is small showing someone of an introvert nature but it slopes upwards indicating he is both optimistic and forward looking." As he spoke, Dr. Schermann walked back and forth and his gait began to change. The animated fellow who began the lecture seemed to disappear to be replaced by a more ponderous man. His voice too changed, became lower in tone, and his German accent all but left him to be replaced by the reserved tones of an English gentleman. We were all astonished by the visible and audible transformation that was taking place.

He continued, as if impersonating someone we could not identify, "The letters are closely spaced and the writer is insecure about his own opinions. I could say more about the slant of the letters, the connecting strokes and a particularly abnormal stroke by which the first letter is linked to the second."

Then he walked back to a large man in the front row and handed him the paper, saying, "But instead I will say that the man who wrote this, the man who likes order so much that he is prepared to spend his days cataloguing life itself, is a librarian. And that librarian is you."

The man took the paper, read it quickly and then rose from his seat and exclaimed, "By God, it's true. He's describing me. I work in the museum archives."

The audience applauded wildly. It was a bravura performance but what exactly did it mean? Had Schermann really been able to see all that in the librarian's handwriting?

"There's more to this impish man than meets the eye, eh, Watson?" said Holmes. I was about to agree when the doctor, who had now regained his former posture, called for quiet.

He looked at the librarian and said, "We are here to talk about criminals, and you, sir, are not a criminal. I know it from your handwriting. You are not a stealer of library books."

As the audience laughed, he took the remaining three papers from the hat and unfolded them. As he looked at them he once again commenced his pacing. Again his voice changed. His accent took on the aspect of a tradesman. "'Riting ain't my game. Didn't go to school. Had no time for it. Was earning my keep other ways. Dark ways. Can't keep to the straight and narrow. But you'll find no finer felon in London."

As he loped from one side of the room to the other he threw two of the papers away and continued his uncanny imitation

45

of the bemused Spring's accent. Then there were gasps from the audience as Dr. Schermann visibly became taller. At first I could not believe it but the reaction from the audience told me that my observation was correct. His small frame was stretching upwards and he now walked several inches taller than when he began. His head sank upon his chest, just like Spring's and his arms no longer moved gracefully but were stiff as if long sticks filled his sleeves. As he came to a halt beside Richard Spring even Lestrade was dumbfounded as he now looked directly into the eyes of the man who moments ago was shorter than he.

"I fink this is yours," said Dr. Schermann, as he handed the last paper to Spring. Spring looked back as if gazing into a mirror and then took the paper. He read the contents and then with a nod of his head admitted that the writing was his. The audience applauded louder than before and as the majority stood to show their approval the platform was temporarily hidden from our sight. By the time Holmes and I stood Dr. Schermann seemed to be his normal self, shorter than Lestrade and enjoying the praise of his peers.

Henry Bloom came forward and announced that Dr. Schermann would remain to take questions from the audience. Lestrade led Richard Spring away into the arms of two burly constables and the criminal's brief outing was over. Holmes made his way to the doors and I followed. We crossed the museum foyer and were almost at the exit when a voice called out from behind us.

"I do believe it is the great Sherlock Holmes and his Boswell, Dr. Watson."

"And would that be London's foremost expert on homicidal maniacs? said Holmes sarcastically without so much as glancing at the man. I knew what Holmes meant and turned around to be greeted by Mr. George Sims, the self-proclaimed expert on 'Jack the Ripper'.

"I'm surprised, Holmes, that you weren't on that podium today," said Sims.

"Instead of whom?" said Holmes, "Dr. Schermann, Lestrade or Richard Spring?"

"Schermann of course," Sims took a cigarette case from his pocket as if expecting to remain for a long conversation, but Holmes anticipated Sims's curiosity, patted him on the arm and said, "Very good to see you, Sims, but we must go. Perhaps you'll come to see me in Baker Street and we can discuss 'Jack the Ripper'?"

For a moment Sims was silenced and before he could utter another word Holmes had spun around and was quickly walking towards the exit.

"Goodbye," I said to Sims and shook him by the hand before following Holmes into the daylight. As I exited I heard Sims call out, "Tell Holmes I will call upon him very soon."

"I will," I said, waving a hand and making my way through the museum's huge doors.

Holmes was waiting in the museum courtyard for me.

"I'm afraid Sims may want to interview you, on the matter of the Mayfair murders."

"I've no time for the likes of Sims. He trades in misery. As of this afternoon I have someone more important to see."

"Are you going to visit Lestrade?"

"No, Watson. On the contrary, I am going to visit our friend Richard Spring. I believe he has something of great interest to us."

A moment later he strode away, blowing on a whistle and hailing a hansom.

Chapter Seven

I spent the remainder of the afternoon at Baker Street in quiet meditation turning over the events of the afternoon in my mind. Mrs. Hudson brought up a pot of Darjeeling and some toasted teacakes, which she thought might take the edge off a hungry stomach. She was right. I had eaten nothing since breakfast. Then I turned to the stack of newspapers I had saved in order to reread the articles concerning the recent events in Mayfair. As least, that is what I had intended but when I opened the newspapers I was astonished to find that the relevant pages had already been removed by Holmes and the rest cut to tatters as countless articles had been clipped. When he did this I do not know, perhaps in the middle of the night, for Holmes slept at irregular hours. A glance at his shelves revealed a new scrapbook, and I took it down and laid it upon the table.

The book was meticulously laid out as was Holmes's fashion and from it emerged the odour of fresh gum. It contained all the newspaper reports of the so called Mayfair murders and a great deal more, including hand-written references to other of Holmes's notebooks, in which I found a number of articles concerning Dr. Schermann and his extraordinary methods.

For the next few hours I studied the scrapbook in order to familiarise myself with the details of the crime. A map of

Mayfair was pasted to the inside cover and Holmes had marked the points at which the first three murders had taken place. The victims were young women in their twenties and each was strangled. One of the women seemed to have put up a struggle and was beaten before being finally subdued and killed. The other two were taken completely by surprise, and their deaths, according to the police report, were almost instantaneous. They could hardly have known what had happened to them.

There were some points of particular interest. None of the women actually lived in the Mayfair area. The first resided in East London, the second in Southwark and the third in St. John's Wood. One was a barmaid at a public house near Piccadilly, one a maid at the Dorchester Hotel and the last a shop girl in Bond Street. Other than the proximity of their employment to the area in which they were found dead, there seemed to be no obvious connection between them. All appeared to be hard working young women of previously good character trying to make a life for themselves in the metropolis. How they came to such a bad end was a mystery.

The only common factor was that these three young ladies had been strangled by an unknown assailant and left for dead on the streets of Mayfair, one of London's most respected districts. This morning a fourth would be added to that list and the details pasted into Holmes's scrapbook. There was much to tie the murders together: the similarities of the victims, the method of execution and the location of their deaths. No doubt the police had held back some vital information as is customary in these matters but of the general picture I thought I had learned as much as was possible.

I was mulling these matters over when I glanced over to Holmes's bedroom door, which lay partly open. There was something subtly different about the light in the room beyond. I walked over to it and pushed the door ajar and was astonished at the sight that confronted me; the walls of his room were covered in a patchwork of newspaper. Tiny clippings, long columns and entire pages were pasted upon the walls. I examined them closely and discovered that they were the personal columns from all of London's newspapers. Lost pets, get-rich-quick schemes, long-lost friends, herbal remedies, items for sale – a potpourri of print depicting a myriad problems and a host of dubious solutions. The papers from which these cuttings had been taken lay scattered all over the room like an enormous black and white counterpane. Holmes had marked some of the advertisements in red ink. He'd underlined names and dates, and appended notes written in his usual scrawl. Upon further examination I could see what he was doing. It was common practice for those who wished to remain anonymous to use codes and ciphers when placing their notices. Lovers sent their plaintive notes this way. Even criminals had been known to use the agony columns when they wished to pass a message to one of their clan. Often the ciphers were childishly simple and easily decoded. One gang of thieves simply wrote their entire message backwards giving the location of their next robbery. Naturally, they were apprehended when the notice was drawn to the attention of the police.

Holmes's writing indicated that he had been searching the advertisements for such ciphers, rearranging words and phrases in order to discover whether another meaning lay beneath them. One message stood out from the rest. He had drawn a circle boldly around it. It read:

Young lady newly arrived in London
wishes to meet similar lady for friendship.

It was signed by a 'Jean Tillett'. Holmes had rearranged the letters of the name into a new order and arrived at 'Jane Little'. The name, of course, was familiar. She was the first of the Mayfair murderer's victims.

I was about to examine the advertisement further when I heard a familiar tread upon the stairs. I hurried back to the lounge, took my place at the table and mustered an air of nonchalance. The door opened, Holmes breezed in and he

51

began to take off his coat. He glanced at the scrapbook before me.

"Ah, I see you have been doing a little detective work of your own, Watson."

"Yes, I thought it would be good to know just what it is we are about." I said nothing of my visit to his room.

"Well, I would certainly like to hear what you make of this curious case, but first I think we are about to have a visit from Mrs. Hudson. I could smell a delicious steak and kidney pie as I took the stairs and I believe our supper is about to arrive." As he sat down to warm his hands at the fire Mrs. Hudson knocked on the door and announced that supper was indeed ready.

The steak and kidney pie and the plum pudding that followed occupied us for the next hour until we finally held a brandy each and took our seats by the fire in order to discuss the case more comfortably.

"Tell me, Watson: you've read as much as I about the murders; what do you make of them?"

"Curious," I said, "one common factor appears to be the manner of their deaths. None of the first three victims knew the others, and none appears to have any reason for being singled out for murder. If the fourth woman was strangled by the same man, I think we'll find that she also had no knowledge of the others. Random murder by a maniac I'd say. Much the same as 'Jack the Ripper'." I knew this not to be true. The papers in Holmes's room indicated a less than random killing, but it was my way of trying to persuade him to open up about what he knew.

Holmes swirled the brandy in his glass, gazing into it as if it were a crystal ball.

"I think I would agree that the killer is deranged in some way; which killer is not? But I'm not sure about your comparison with the 'Ripper' murders."

"But what other motive could there be," I said. "These are random attacks of violence visited upon innocent women. In that respect the similarity to the 'Ripper' murders seems obvious."

"Watson, you leap ahead of yourself. To begin with, we do not know what motivated 'Jack the Ripper' since he was never caught. Of course, to us the murders looked random, but who can tell what the murders meant to the fiend himself? The insane see chaos where we see order, but they can also perceive order where only chaos exists. Did 'Jack' murder whores because it suited some fine plan he had, or because they were vulnerable? We do not know. And did the subject of our present discussion really choose four ladies at random or had he chosen them because of some peculiar quality of their manner, or dress, or even the scent that they wore."

"We don't know," I said. "Who can tell what possessed the man?"

"Precisely," responded Holmes, "and we won't know until we catch the murderer. Which brings me to another point. You have twice now referred to the murderer as a man. What brought you to that conclusion, Watson?"

"Several things. First it is a fact that the majority of murderers are men. All four women were strangled with such ferocity and strength that only a man could bring to bear. When a women kills it is apt to be by a knife, gun or poison, but strangulation is, I venture, virtually unknown to the sex. And, finally, one woman was beaten badly, again indicating a strength that could only exist within a male assailant." I felt I'd made a good and logical case, just as Holmes might, and could not imagine how he hoped to counter it.

"Very good, Watson, and I won't disagree with a word of it. However, it does beg the question as to why any of these ladies would walk with a man who appears to be a total stranger to them. These were not whores; they were respectable working women – a shop girl, a young lady in the employment of one of the city's finest hotels, and another who worked at one of London's most convivial hostelries. I dare say the fourth will turn out to be of similar character. If the reports are correct we also know that two were single and one was engaged to be married. Not the type to seek the company of strange men, I think you will agree. And yet a man unknown to them, a murderous villain, managed to pick them out of the crowded streets of London and strangle them. How did he do this?"

I had to admit that Holmes had once again hit upon the crux of the matter. Under what circumstances did these innocent women meet their assailant? I thought again of the advertisement fixed to the wall and took a sip of brandy as I pondered the point further, and then another as no useful thoughts presented themselves.

"What we need to establish," said Holmes, "is the relationship of the last person to see the victim. The murderer could, as you rightly point out, have been totally unknown to any of the ladies, but I have to say that this is rare, most victims have some connection with their murderers. My instincts tell me that these women walked with their murderer, perhaps even talked with him before he ended their young lives. They went willingly with him to their deaths. Only one victim struggled before she was killed and I'll wager that was because she had anticipated his murderous intentions."

"Unfortunately she was too late."

"I'm afraid so," said Holmes. "Let us hope that we are not."

Holmes finished his brandy in silence. Often he would solve a crime by contemplating the actions of the perpetrator. He could think like the lowest thief or the master criminal and anticipate their every action as if he too were possessed of a criminal mind. But as he gazed at the fire through his empty glass I got the impression that on this occasion he was not thinking like the criminal at all. No, he was placing himself in the mind of the victim trying to envisage the circumstances under which a lamb is led willingly to slaughter.

"More brandy, Holmes?" I said, preparing myself to ask him about the clippings upon his bedroom walls.

"No thank you, Watson," he said. "Let me tell you about my afternoon."

"Yes, where did you go after the lecture?" I muttered, surprised that the conversation was about to take a different turn.

"To visit Richard Spring," Holmes replied. "Lestrade took Spring back to Wormwood Scrubs. I waited until he left and then went inside pretending to be on some official business."

"And what business was that?"

"They never asked, so fortunately I never had to say," said Holmes laughing.

"And just what did you discover from the slippery Spring?" I asked.

"This," said Holmes, and he took a slip of paper from his pocket and placed it on the table. "It is the secret of Schermann's psycho-graphology."

Chapter Eight

I put my brandy glass aside and took the paper from Holmes. It looked quite ordinary save for three words written across one side, 'The game's afoot'.

I read them aloud, "The game's afoot. I see Spring is not as uneducated as he appears."

"Quite so," said Holmes, "The game's afoot: Follow your spirit; and, upon this charge cry God for Harry, England and Saint George!" and he raised his glass into the air as if making a toast. "Spring has a great affection for Shakespeare and he tells me that *Henry V* is one of his favourites. You know he used to be a teacher long before he became a forger?"

"I had no idea."

"Yes, and he still paints too though does not attempt to sell them under any name but his own. His cell is adorned with the most extraordinary pictures and they are highly sought after by the warders. Spring makes gifts of them and in return the warders make Spring's life a little easier than perhaps it ought to be given his present circumstances."

My image of Spring as some low brow illiterate who merely copied the work of master artists had been rudely crushed but I could not see what this had to do Dr. Shermann and said so. As Holmes placed his glass on the table I knew immediately that I had once again fallen into one of his traps of reasoning.

"Simple," said Holmes, "you mistook Spring for an uneducated man. So did Dr. Schermann. What did Schermann's much-vaunted psycho-graphology determine from Spring's handwriting? That he 'had no time for writing' and 'didn't go to school'. Wrong on both counts. Not only is Spring fully conversant with our greatest playwright but it appears that Dr. Schermann is not, otherwise he would have recognised Spring's quotation. Had he done so he would also have realised that Spring is not as uneducated as he appears. Spring had a fine education and was by all accounts an outstanding pupil. He also taught art at one of London's finest private schools though, as you will appreciate, this is not something they boast about."

"Then Schermann's techniques are flawed," I added.

"No, they are not flawed. They are sheer nonsense. As bogus as the art that put Richard Spring where he is today."

Holmes was in fine form and enjoying every minute of it. It was good to have the old Holmes back and I sat there with eager anticipation knowing that there were more revelations to come. As for Holmes, his face positively shone with an inner glow that came not from the brandy but from knowledge and the pleasure he always got telling what he knew. The game was indeed afoot and, despite being a latecomer to the party, Holmes knew he had the advantage.

Unable to stand the suspense any longer, I asked Holmes for more details, "But if Dr. Schermann's methods don't work then how was he able to identify Spring from the writing on this paper?"

"He didn't," said Holmes.

"But he did. He clearly pointed out that the man who wrote this note was the criminal and Spring was the only criminal among them."

"I beg to differ. Dr. Schermann identified nothing from this writing because there is nothing in this writing that gives Spring away. Indeed, as I have already pointed out, Schermann's analysis of Spring's character was totally wrong. He had mistakenly thought him to be no more than a common thief."

I examined the paper, more closely this time, noting the slope of the letters and trying to remember what Schermann had said about it. There was something familiar about the handwriting but without Schermann to guide me it was nothing more than a meaningless set of loops and lines. I was about to interrupt again but Holmes, seeing my dilemma, continued.

"Dr. Schermann identified Spring not from the writing but from the paper."

"You mean fingerprints?" I asked and held the paper up to the light of the fire to take a closer look. I didn't really know what I was looking for. Maybe a smudge of ink, or a smear of grease. Something. Try as I might, though, I saw nothing. It was just a sheet of paper with Spring's writing across it.

"Let me show you," said Holmes, taking the paper from me and laying it upon the table. "Where did this paper come from?"

I looked again at the paper and tried to recall the lecture. I remembered that it was Henry Bloom, surely a man above suspicion, who had produced the paper. It was a large sheet, which he tore into four pieces before handing a piece to each of the four volunteers. One of those pieces went to Richard Spring. Then I looked at the paper again as it lay on the table, the writing facing me.

I could see the torn edges running along the left hand side and along the bottom. The top edge and the right hand side of the paper were straight, having been cut by a guillotine. It was, like most tricks, diabolically simple but it took a few moments to realise what had happened.

Holmes now produced a sheet of paper of his own, saying, "I see you have the solution Watson," and he proceeded to fold the sheet into half. He tore the sheet into two along the crease, put the half-sheets together, creased them down the middle and tore them again to produce four quarters. These he lay across the table. Now the method was obvious. Each quarter had its torn edges in a different place. Dr. Schermann only had to note which quarter Spring received and he would be able to identify it later.

"It is incredibly simple but not without risk," said Holmes. "Schermann has to be sure that no one turns their papers over or end for end or that would spoil the arrangement."

"But he didn't turn his back on them until they had begun to write," I said.

"And I'm sure that the Doctor has a few more tricks up his sleeve should this method fail," said Holmes. "The position of the watermark on the paper could also give away its owner."

I shuffled the papers around on the table just to be sure that Holmes's theory about the torn edges was true. Holmes was right. There were any number of ways of identifying the paper that did not depend on so-called psycho-graphology. It was hard to credit that such a simple piece of legerdemain had duped not only Henry Bloom and his fellow academics at the British Museum but the officers of Scotland Yard and Europe's leading police forces.

"I can hardly believe that such a ruse could go undetected," I said.

"But it can and it has. Men look for complexity where simplicity would suffice. If I'm not mistaken, even you were taken in, Watson."

I had to confess that I was. It had all sounded so plausible. So exciting. But it was no more credible than astrology or the philosophies of the Spiritualists. I regretted that the adventure had come to an end before it had begun and wondered how long it would be before Holmes sank back into his depression. All that remained was for us to reveal Schermann's trickery to Lestrade and watch with some delight as the rogue was sent packing back across the Channel to explain himself to the Continental police authorities who, I dare say, would not be as forgiving as their British counterparts. I asked Holmes as to when he would inform Lestrade of his discovery.

"Tomorrow morning. The sooner Schermann is unmasked the quicker a real investigation into the Mayfair murders can begin."

To my astonishment he poured himself another brandy and topped up my glass too. He seemed to be in a rare humour and leaned back in his chair planning something that, for the moment at least, he could not share. For several minutes we sat quietly, sipping our brandies and gazing into the warm fire. I mused on the events of the day and how convincingly Schermann had given his performance. Once the trick with the paper was explained the surrounding theatrics were less impressive. Schermann was undoubtedly a skilled mimic; able to impersonate those around him as if reflecting the personalities he claimed were imbued in the handwriting. And although I wasn't sure how he was able to stretch himself to Spring's height I felt nevertheless that it was some simple trick that Holmes would explain in his own time. I was thinking about this illusion when Holmes leant forward and pushed Spring's paper towards me.

"One final thing. Whose writing is that?"

I was puzzled by Holmes's question and thought we had already established that it was Richard Spring who wrote the Shakespearian quotation. "I'm not sure what you mean Holmes," I said, "Didn't you say you got the paper from Richard Spring?"

"Yes I did. But you forget that Spring is a master forger. He hasn't signed his own signature to anything for years. He certainly didn't sign this in his own handwriting."

I looked at the paper and the familiarity that had struck me before groped for meaning. "I'm not sure. It does look familiar. Whose signature did Spring use?"

Holmes picked the paper up from the table and laughed. "Spring likes a joke. He copied the handwriting of the officer who signed him out of prison this morning," said Holmes.

"And who would that be?" I asked.

Holmes laughed again. "Why it's our friend Lestrade," he said, "dear old Lestrade."

Chapter Nine

Holmes's visit with Lestrade had not gone well and he returned home in a foul mood.

"The damn fools," said Holmes. "They are nothing more than sheep and their shepherd is a woman no less."

I imagined Little Bo Peep leading Lestrade around but wisely kept the thought to myself. It was just as well. Holmes was in no mood for humour.

He had explained Dr. Schermann's trick believing that Lestrade would immediately have him arrested or, at the very least, detained. To Holmes's surprise he did neither. Nor was he amused, or astonished, to find that the demonstration at the British Museum had been a trick. In fact he had taken offence at Holmes's suggestion that he would be fooled by such an enterprise. No, the problem he explained was far more complex than that for Dr. Schermann was here in England at the behest of Sir Edward Bradford, the Commissioner of the Metropolitan Police. And that, as far as he was concerned, was an end to the matter. One did not question one's superior, particularly when his wife, was so fond of Dr. Schermann. Holmes was advised to forget all about the Mayfair murders. It was a police matter and nothing more.

"It's politics; that's what it is, Watson," said Holmes fuming, "and I'm done with them all."

As I listened to Holmes's account, the ghost of Abbey Grange once again came to mind and I wondered whether we would ever be forgiven.

That was the last I heard from Holmes on the matter. His depression returned and it made him powerless to take an interest in anything except the murders, the details of which consumed him. For the next few days he slept little and ate at irregular hours, that was if he ate at all. I too began to feel the effects of Holmes's depleted energies. As his friend and physician I recommended that we both leave London and spend a few days away from its choking fogs, ignorant hysteria, Lestrade and Dr. Schermann. To my astonishment, he agreed with my remedy and we set off for a short convalescence on the south coast of England, Eastbourne to be precise.

We travelled by train but spent most of the journey in silence, Holmes reading the collection of papers he had purchased at the station while I made some notes in my journal, or at least pretended to. In fact I scribbled idly, my mind occupied with the view of England's landscape from our carriage window. As we passed the fallow acres that made up this seemingly endless space, I could not help but compare the countryside with the claustrophobia of London. Holmes, on the other hand, barely looked out of his window and when he did it was to draw the blind because the sun was in his eyes.

The journey was singularly uneventful and the train arrived on time. We took rooms at The Esplanade Hotel and after a brief rest arranged to meet in the lounge and begin our exploration of Eastbourne from there. It was not the holiday season but many shops and restaurants were still open and there was more than enough to distract us. It was cold but not cold enough to prevent us taking a bench at the end of Eastbourne's marvellous pier and just sitting in silence to watch the gentle roll of the incoming waves as high tide approached. Behind us stretched the promenade and behind that a line of white painted hotels, standing shoulder to shoulder and gazing out at the sea like Easter Island statues.

With the cold tide lapping beneath our feet we breathed in the fine air and sat in quiet contemplation.

Occasionally a ship would drift by on the horizon, marking time like the minute hand of a clock as it crossed our view. There was nothing to do save watch the ocean and listen to the gulls as they circled overhead, and I was enjoying every slow minute of it. But while I was relaxing my companion was bored and restless. The ghosts of Mayfair had not been entirely banished. He fidgeted constantly, folding and unfolding his arms when not filling or emptying his pipe and fouling the salt air with its noxious fumes. It was as if he had tried to bring the smog of London with him. At frequent intervals he would reach into his pocket, bring out a notebook and mark some detail upon its page, no doubt a memorandum for some task to be done when he returned to Baker Street. He seemed out of sorts with the easy pace of life that surrounded him and yet he made no complaint. Whenever I asked how much he was enjoying our time away he would merely say how different it was to be out of the city and then light up another pipe of tobacco.

At about seven o'clock we decided to take a late supper at a local public house, The Anchor. The porter at our hotel had recommended it and Holmes said that it might give us a better impression of the local way of life that I had become so fond of, but I suspected that once again he was trying to find something that would remind him of London. He had chosen well. The interior, even on a bright day such as this, was dark. Mahogany panelling soaked up the light and gave out only shadows in return. Nets and lobster pots hung from the ceiling and ageing photographs and sombre paintings of life at sea decorated the walls. A long bar took up one side of the room and a knot of men stood against it, all locals, not the sort you see promenading along the front or taking the air on the pier, but friendly enough all the same. We ordered our drinks and a meal, and although the fare was limited we managed to choose something that appealed and then we wandered over to one of the dining tables set along the opposite wall.

When the meal did arrive it was most welcome and, I have

to confess, delicious. It was a far cry from the delicate servings offered at our hotel and I'm sure it only served to remind Holmes of Mrs. Hudson's cooking … and Baker Street … and London … and, of course, Dr. Schermann.

At the end of supper the landlord surprised us by bringing forth a fine brandy that put us both in a mellow mood. We sat quietly content, watching a group of fishermen furrow their tawny brows in concentration as they played a game of darts. The tap, tap, tapping of their arrows as they struck the board had the same soporific effect as the waves we watched lapping the shore.

As uncomplaining as Holmes was, I was nevertheless aware that the south coast might be proving to be less than stimulating for his agile mind, and in an attempt to engage his interest I asked what he would like to do tomorrow.

"I think that has already been decided for us," he said glancing over my shoulder. I turned around and saw a portly man walking towards us. He looked as if he had been running, an exercise for which he was not well prepared, and his face was as bright as a tomato. He wore a dark well-made suit for which he appeared to be a size too large and carried a leather briefcase in his arms.

"Have I the pleasure of addressing Mr. Holmes?" he gasped.

"You do," said Holmes, "and this is my colleague Dr. Watson. What brings you so urgently from your work."

The man looked puzzled. "My work?"

"Yes, surely the presses cannot roll without you. You are the editor of the local newspaper are you not?"

"Why yes. I'm sorry, have we already met?"

"Just a moment ago. I introduced myself and Watson but as yet we do not have the benefit of knowing your name. Please, sit down and perhaps you can introduce yourself properly."

The man drew up a chair and laid his briefcase to one side then he pulled out a handkerchief to mop his sweated brow. "Well I have read much about your powers, Mr. Holmes, in your articles, Dr. Watson, but I never imagined for one minute that they were so, so …"

"Accurate," I said, trying to be helpful.

"That's the word. Accurate. You were spot on, Mr. Holmes. I am the editor of *The Eastbourne Herald* but how could you have known that?"

"I didn't," said Holmes, "at least I didn't know it was *The Eastbourne Herald*. I believe there are two newspapers in Eastbourne – isn't that so?"

The man nodded his agreement, "But still, to be so, so …"

"Discerning," I suggested. "Discerning, right that'll do. So discerning. It's almost supernatural."

"Not at all," said Holmes. "You are obviously a well dressed fellow and well fed too if you'll pardon me for saying so. What would a wealthy man like yourself be doing with printer's ink on his hands?"

The man held his hands up and turned them over. Holmes was right. Black smudges stained the thumb and fingers. As our new acquaintance tried to wipe the ink away with his handkerchief Holmes continued to share his deductions. "Either you read a lot of newspapers or have just read one that was freshly printed, and having done so were not able to wash. I concluded that you read the papers at work and as it was getting rather late I decided that you must be in the printing business. And if you did not have an opportunity to wash the print from your fingers then I warrant you did not have the chance to change your clothes either. What kind of man wears a suit to a printworks and a fine suit at that? The editor and proprietor was my conclusion and I'm happy to say that you've proved me right."

"Well, well, Mr. Holmes, that was quite, quite …"

"Marvellous?" I offered.

"Astounding, I was going to say. I'd shake your hand but for the ink."

"Consider it shaken," said Holmes. "Now perhaps you'd like to join us in a brandy and tell us why you have sought me out?"

Chapter Ten

Our flustered visitor was Benjamin Crane, the editor and sole proprietor of *The Eastbourne Herald*, a rather slim newspaper with a circulation as faltering as that of its red-faced owner. As the editor, it was his business to know who was in town, and, on his making further enquiries, the porter at The Esplanade Hotel had directed him to The Anchor where, he was told, the great Sherlock Holmes would be enjoying supper. He took a brandy, spent a few moments composing himself and then began his tale.

"They are trying to run me out of town, Mr. Holmes! They've chased away one printer and now they are trying to chase away my new man, and very good he is too. I'll never find another. I've been here five years Mr. Holmes, five years. Why ..."

Holmes raised a hand and Crane's babbling immediately ceased. "Slowly man, slowly. Start at the beginning. We have plenty of time; we're here for the rest of the week, aren't we, Watson?" I saw the mischief in Holmes's eye but nodded my agreement all the same.

Crane began again but I feel bound to protect the reader from his, often incoherent, ramblings by paraphrasing his erratic account. He had lived in Eastbourne for the past five years and, having purchased *The Eastbourne Herald* from the previous proprietor, he had made himself editor. As well as the paper he had taken on Mr Bernard Evans, the paper's printer. Evans seemed happy enough working under Mr. Crane until one day in July when two men visited Evans at the newspaper's offices. The printer wouldn't say what it was about; indeed he said little to Crane after that. One week later he was gone, not only from the newspaper but from Eastbourne. He had simply vanished.

Benjamin Crane was distraught although he seemed to be more concerned over the lack of a printer, any printer, than the disappearance of Evans or his fate. He placed an advertisement in the national press and a day later employed a young man called Davis. Davis was a fine printer, even more efficient than Evans, but several weeks ago two men had turned up at the newspaper's offices and asked to speak with him. They were the same two men who had spoken to Evans some months before. They called on Davis each week, always on the same day.

"What am I to do?" said Crane. "They are going to chase him away – I know it."

"Why on earth would they do that?" I asked.

"Yes," said Holmes, "why do you assume that someone is trying to persuade your printer to leave? Evans may have left Eastbourne for an entirely different reason. Granted his sudden departure is strange but it may have no connection with the meeting you observed."

"The articles, Mr. Holmes. There are certain parties on the council who would be glad to see my newspaper closed. But I defy them all. I'll print what I like and be damned!"

Crane reached into his briefcase and brought out a selection of newspaper cuttings, which he spread across the table. For a moment I thought we would see Dr. Schermann's name printed on every one. Gingerly I picked up one of the cuttings, as did Holmes. Fortunately Dr. Schermman's exploits had not made *The Eastbourne Herald* and it wasn't long before we understood the gist of Mr. Crane's story and made sense of his paranoia.

The articles accused a local businessman, Mr. Samuel Randlett, of attempting to enlarge his empire of seafront hotels by bribing local councillors and using his considerable influence in Eastbourne to the enhancement of himself and the detriment of others. The stories were indeed provocative and if the allegations were true then Randlett was a man to be watched, and Crane not quite the bumbling fellow he first appeared.

"If these allegations are true why have the local authorities not acted upon them?" said Holmes.

"They are afraid. Randlett owns many of the prime tourist sites in Eastbourne. You can't sit on the promenade, stroll along the pier or visit the bandstand without paying homage to him. He owns many of the gift shops and more than his fair share of hotels. Don't misunderstand me. I don't object to a man owning half the town if he got it fairly, but Randlett doesn't do anything fairly. He has a gang of thugs who make life difficult for those who refuse to sell. The same thugs that threatened Bernard Evans and are now threatening poor Davis. And I'll not stand for it."

It seemed to me that there was too much supposition in Crane's story balanced only by a distinct lack of evidence. To date no one had come forward and accused Randlett of any crime. Not even the people whose businesses he had bought. Even Davis had said nothing. Only Crane seemed to see the Devil where others saw a great entrepreneur, a man who was making Eastbourne one of the country's most popular seaside resorts.

"It is indeed a mixed bag," I said, "I appreciate your worries, Mr. Crane, but where exactly is the crime?"

Crane looked at me astonished. "Why, it has not happened yet, but I tell you it will. Davis will disappear, my newspaper will close and Randlett will be left to buy up Eastbourne unchecked. There's the crime."

He started to pick up the cuttings from the table and put them back into his briefcase. The sorry look on his face made me consider my own motives for rejecting his story out of hand. It had taken a great deal of effort to persuade Holmes to come to Eastbourne and perhaps I felt threatened that our time here was about to come to a premature conclusion. In

71

contrast Holmes's countenance had brightened considerably since Crane's arrival.

"Watson's right. We appreciate your situation but we have nothing more substantial than candyfloss. If I'm to take the case I need a fact."

Crane looked hopeful. "Yes, anything. If you'll just give me a little of your time I'll be so, so …"

"Grateful," I offered.

"Indeed. Very grateful."

Holmes pressed his fingertips together and brought them to his chin as if in prayer. He thought for a moment and then said, "Are you absolutely sure that the men who visited Davis are in Randlett's employ?"

"They are hired thugs, you can tell as much by looking at them. They are often seen around town and I have heard that they are nothing but trouble for the local shopkeepers and publicans. You can see for yourself, Mr Holmes, because if they are keeping to schedule they'll be visiting Davis tomorrow afternoon. Come, join me – you too, Dr. Watson – and be the judge."

Holmes looked at me as if seeking my acquiescence. Even the hint of a crime had sent a spark dancing behind his grey eyes and a ghost of a smile could be seen across his thin lips. An adventure was in the offing but he would not take it without my permission. I turned to Crane who waited anxiously on Holmes's words. There were few things I could do for Holmes as a physician but there was much I could do as his friend. Our holiday had come to an end but our adventure had just begun.

Chapter Eleven

The following morning the weather had taken a turn for the worse. It was much colder, and a heavy breeze was blowing in from the sea and brought the threat of rain. We took breakfast at the hotel and, having been duly fortified, and wrapped in our thickest coats, we walked to the *The Eastbourne Herald* offices at the town centre where we had arranged to meet Benjamin Crane. He met us at the main entrance to the building and then took us inside and gave us a tour of the premises. It was the day after publication and was, like most newspaper offices, empty. I had visited Fleet Street and watched the great printing presses cranking out thousands of newspapers, and I had imagined that this enterprise would be something similar. I was wrong. The entire staff consisted of Crane, one secretary, a reporter, a typesetter and Davis his printer. Davis would arrive later to tend to his machine, but the secretary and typesetter wouldn't be needed until morning, and the reporter was away covering the story of a fishing vessel which had ran aground further along the coast.

The press itself lay in a print room separate from the offices. It was much smaller than I had imagined, about chest high in fact, a mechanical marvel of steel drums and pistons that turned plain paper into newsprint in the twinkling of an eye. "The previous proprietor had it installed," said Crane, who was justly proud of his machinery.

"It's a Miehle," said Holmes, who was clearly impressed. "I didn't know there were any in Europe."

"I believe this is the only one," said Crane, "my predecessor was a close acquaintance of the inventor, Robert Miehle. It's quite revolutionary."

"Remarkably clean too," observed Holmes, "You'd hardly believe you were in the newspaper business." The office was indeed one of best kept I had ever seen. Fresh paper was neatly stacked in rolls at one end of the room, ink carefully arranged in large tubs at the other, floor freshly swept and the machinery looking as new and as shiny as the day it was delivered.

"That's all down to Davis," said Crane. "This is one of the best and most modern printing presses in the south of England and Davis is one of the finest printers. He works long hours and must be the tidiest man alive. I get more ink on me reading the paper than he gets printing it."

Holmes knelt down and looked into the maze of gears and pulleys inside the press. "How long does it take to produce an edition of your newspaper?"

"Most of the week. We finished the last of the sheets yesterday and it was delivered last night."

"And Davis delivers the paper too?"

"Oh no. It's collected by our distributor Tom Sutton. I have a wagon at the coach house, and when he's not distributing the papers he's looking after the horses. He deals with deliveries. After we've gone to press Davis cleans up, goes home, takes a well-earned rest and then we start all over again. He has the morning off but will be in at two o'clock."

Holmes examined several coarsely woven sacks in the corner of the room. Opening them he found the misprinted runoffs that Davis had produced when printing last night's Herald. "And do you have cleaners to take away the waste paper?"

"I used to but not any more. Davis does that too. He bags it up and then burns it near Beachy Head. I haven't seen a shred of rubbish since I employed him."

Holmes stood up and walked over to the pots of coloured ink and examined them one by one as he talked.

"You said that the thugs will visit Davis this afternoon. Is there somewhere we can watch them unobserved?"

"Indeed there is," said Crane, "I had the very same idea myself. Come this way." He took us to his private office adjacent to the print room. The door opened with the most awful squeak.

"Seems to need some oil," I said.

"I oil it every week but it does no good. I think the hinges are twisted. Davis said he'd sort it out and I dare say he will when he has time."

The office contained a writing desk, some cabinets and hundreds of files. Bundles of paper tied with twine were stacked up in the corners of the room and an assortment of books, mostly on legal matters, were scattered across the floor like stepping-stones.

"I see that Davis's neatness stops at your threshold," said Holmes.

"Yes this is my domain. It may look a terrible mess but every sheet of paper tells a story, and not one that Randlett cares to hear, I can tell you."

Opposite us was a door that led to the street. Crane went over to it and turned the handle to make sure it was locked. Then he returned to the wall that separated the office from the print room. On it were a number of frames all containing vintage editions of *The Eastbourne Herald*. He pressed his hand against the first and it slid easily to one side revealing a tiny peephole. "I had this put in last week," he said. "I wouldn't normally spy on my employees but what else was I to do?"

Suddenly I was beginning to feel a little uncomfortable at the unwavering determination with which Mr. Crane pursued his case and I wondered whether it was all in his imagination and this chaotic office represented his confused state of mind.

But those doubts vanished entirely as the afternoon came upon us to be replaced with some confusion of my own.

At two o'clock Holmes, Mr. Crane and I were hidden in his office peering through a series of holes that were usually hidden behind the frames on the wall. I must confess that I felt very foolish. Crane had locked the door adjoining the print room so that we would not be interrupted. Davis arrived on time. He was a young man with a pale face and shaggy mop of ginger hair on his head. In his right hand he carried a canvas knapsack, which he laid on the table next to the inks. He walked to the printing press and looked it over, examining the roller mechanism and paper feed with great care. All this took some considerable time so Crane and I left our posts while Holmes kept watch. Now and then Holmes would whisper some detail that he thought interesting. Suddenly we heard the sound of the heavy footsteps and he waved us over. Once again we took up our positions as covert observers.

Two men walked in. They appeared to be every bit as thuggish as Crane had suggested. One was tall and lean, the other shorter with a barrel-chest. Both were powerful looking and, although I am not a follower of physiognomy, their scarred and broken faces showed the misspent years and callous lives of hardened criminals. If they had shown up at Evans's door, it was not surprising that he had decided it was time to move on.

Davis on the other hand seemed quite unafraid of them. They said something to him that we could not hear and he reached into his knapsack and pulled out a wallet. He opened it, withdrew a five-pound note and handed it to them. They took it without thanking him and left without saying goodbye. Crane whispered, "Blackmail," and Holmes put a hand on his shoulder to stop him saying more. We moved back from the wall and quietly slid the frames back into place.

Holmes pointed to the door and signalled that we should leave. "We must follow them," he said in hushed tones. Crane unlocked the door to the street and we opened it slowly, hoping that it did not squeak like its brother. Once outside we walked around to the front of the building just in time to see the two men climb into a country trap that was stationed across the road. With a crack of the whip they set off.

Holmes turned to Crane, "Have you transport?"

"I've a four-wheeler at the coach house," he replied.

"Meet us at our hotel," said Holmes.

"Why the hotel?" I asked.

"To pick up your revolver, Watson. I trust you've brought it with you."

A few minutes later I was travelling along a dusty road in a badly sprung open-topped carriage with Holmes by my side, Crane as our driver and a loaded gun in my pocket. It was not the holiday I had imagined.

Chapter Twelve

We travelled for several miles west out of Eastbourne along a narrow road that ran atop the magnificent chalk cliffs that formed the Sussex coastline, always remaining out of sight of our prey. A harsh wind tore at our faces and burned our skin. The sky had begun to darken and I felt sure that rain was less than an hour away. The two thugs were not difficult to follow; having set off along the coast road, their options were limited and their dusty tracks made for an obvious trail.

"I think I know where they are going," shouted Crane from his driver's seat.

"Where?" asked Holmes.

"Belle Tout lighthouse. It's about a mile up the road. There's nothing else along this path."

We had travelled but a few hundred yards more and were driving up a shallow hill when, to our surprise, we heard the sound of a carriage coming in the opposite direction.

"They may have decided to return to town," said Holmes, "if so we will drive on."

When we reached the top of the hill Crane quickly brought the four-wheeler to a stop. "There's the villain," said Crane, and pointed to the driver who approached us. "It's Randlett," he said and before Holmes or I could prevent it he was shouting for the fellow to stop.

Randlett seemed to be in something of a hurry but on seeing Crane he halted his carriage and drew up alongside ours, his sweating horse no doubt grateful for the rest. Randlett looked every inch the prosperous entrepreneur with his fine country tweeds and smart hat. He did not seem at all pleased to see Crane and I got that impression that he might had said something had it not been for our company. Instead it was Crane that spoke first.

"You seem as lathered as your horse, Randlett? Somebody finally caught up with you?"

"I'm sure I don't know what you mean, but I warn you now that if I have to hear any more of your slander, you'll have the law to answer to."

"Your money won't buy my silence, Randlett, and your thugs won't stop my newspaper," said Crane. He was about to say more but Randlett interrupted, "I'm sorry, Benjamin, but I've haven't got time for this, not now. Good day, gentlemen." He nodded to Holmes and I and then took up the reins and started off back to Eastbourne at something of a gallop.

The encounter was brief but Crane tried to make more of it by asking if we could see the villainy in his antagonist's eyes. "I'm afraid not," said Holmes, "perhaps the shade of the hat obstructed my view." I knew he was being amusing at Crane's expense but Crane did not. He worked himself into a state recounting the many evils that Randlett had perpetrated in his commercial activities and once again began to lose his grasp for language, "I'll have the man ..." then stuttered as he tried to finish his sentence. I did not offer to complete it for him.

Holmes was concerned that we were wasting time and asked Crane how far it was to the lighthouse.

"Less than a mile," said Crane.

"Who lives there?"

"No one. It's been abandoned for some time. Erosion, you see. Each year a few feet of the coastline falls into the sea and it won't be long before Belle Tout will go the same way. They're building a new lighthouse down at Beachy Head."

"It might be wise if you remain here and Watson and I will go ahead on foot," said Holmes.

"We might be in for a spot of rain." I pointed to the sky where dark clouds had gathered at the horizon and a strong wind was pushing them inland.

"Dr. Watson's right," said Crane, "I think a storm might be on the way."

"All the better," said Holmes, "we might be able to make use of it."

And so we left Crane on the road tending to his horses while Holmes and I walked on. Neither of us was sorry to leave Crane behind.

The track dipped and then rose again along a crest, the coastline to its left and woodlands to its right. If we had walked any further along the coast or the road we would have been seen so we took to the woods and followed them for the rest of the way. It wasn't long before we saw Belle Tout, a massively solid, stubby brick tower some seventy yards from the cliff edge. At its foot was a low building, probably designed as accommodation for the keeper, and poking out of it was a tall chimney. Smoke drifted out and trailed towards us driven by the ocean winds, which were now getting stronger.

"Crane was right," I said. "They're hiding in the lighthouse. Look! They've lit the fire."

We walked through the woods and around to the other side of the Belle Tout where we saw their horse and trap. The door of the lighthouse was closed. We remained hidden in the woods for some time watching the lighthouse chimney smoke whip across the sky and hoping that someone would open the door but no one did. An hour passed and all that changed was the colour of the sky as the dark clouds passed overhead. Soon the first drops of rain began to fall.

"Should we go back?" I asked.

"No, I think we'll wait a few more minutes and then knock on the door."

Had I not known Holmes well I would have thought he was jesting. Within a few minutes the rain had begun to fall

81

rather heavily and we ran out of the woods towards the lighthouse where, as Holmes had promised, we knocked politely on the door.

It did not open. Instead we heard a scuffling inside and voices. Holmes knocked again and then called out, "Hello. Hello."

He pushed against the door and to our surprise found that it was not locked. "Hello," said Holmes again, as he led the way inside. "I'm sorry to bother you but we've been caught in this dreadful rain."

The door opened on what appeared to be a dining room. It was sparsely furnished with a rough wooden table and two chairs. On the table stood a bottle of whisky and a couple of glasses, both half-full, and against the wall were a number of brown sacks and several brown paper packages stacked one on top of the other. We walked over to them to investigate further, Holmes still calling out and playing his role as the lost tourist while I kept a hand on the revolver in my pocket. As we got to the centre of the room I felt the heat of the fire on my back and turned around to face it. It blazed furiously as if it had just been fuelled. A small stove stood beside it, and beside that was the tall man we had seen in Crane's printroom. He held a battered metal pot in his hand containing beans.

He said nothing and seemed genuinely surprised by our presence. Holmes immediately introduced himself saying, "Ah, there you are. So sorry to intrude, but we got caught in the downpour. I'm Harry Bellamy and this is my friend James Whitmore." Holmes held out his hand and the tall man shook it somewhat uncertainly then set the pot on top of the stove.

"I wonder if we might spend the next few minutes sheltering here, just until the rain passes by. I should think it will be over soon. What do you say, Whitmore?"

Holmes was playing at such a speed that it was a moment or two before I realised that I was Whitmore and that I'd better express my opinion on the weather.

"Yes, yes, er ..." I had not taken in Holmes's new sobriquet, so couldn't use it, and merely finished by agreeing that I was sure the rain would finish soon.

The tall man seemed slightly perplexed by all this. Finally he broke his silence, "Yes, sit yourselves down," and offered us the chairs by the table. He was perspiring and I thought it was as much from nervousness as from the heat of the fire. He called out to his accomplice, "Fred, better come down. We have visitors," and we heard someone walking down the tower stairway.

The second man, a short battle-scarred fellow, walked into the room and eyed us with suspicion. Holmes introduced us once again and this time I made a determined effort to remember my newly given name. I didn't know what plan Holmes had in mind so was content to let him carry the conversation. He walked over to the fireplace and stood before it, drying his damp clothes. "Do you work here, at the lighthouse?" he asked.

It was the short man's turn to talk. "No, the lighthouse is abandoned. We're just here to make sure it's still standing, tidy up a bit and make any repairs that might be necessary."

"Maintenance?" asked Holmes.

"That's right, maintenance."

"And who is the owner of this fine property?"

"Not me, that's for sure," he said with a laugh. His companion joined him, "Yeah, not us, That's for sure," he repeated.

The laughter didn't last long and when it had finished the short man told us that they were just caretakers, checking on the property on behalf of the owners. It wasn't a terribly convincing story.

The fire in the grate had quickly died down leaving only ashes, and the rain outside had stopped as suddenly as it had started. "Well, we'll be on our way then," said Holmes. "Nice to have met you, and thank you for the hospitality. Most kind. Come, James, it's a long way into town."

We were almost at the door when Holmes turned to the short man, "You wouldn't happen to be driving into Eastbourne would you?"

The short man shook his head, "Sorry. Our next appointment is in, er ..."

"Bexhill," offered the tall man.

"Bexhill," repeated the short man.

"Well thank you anyway. Come, James, or we'll miss our tea." And with that we bid our newfound friends farewell and set off down the road towards Eastbourne.

As soon as we were over the crest I told Holmes that I thought he had been a little bold in expecting a ride into Eastbourne.

"I thought so too," he said, "I'm afraid I was just testing the waters. Frankly I don't think they'll be going anywhere tonight."

"What about Bexhill?"

"I'm sure they haven't the faintest notion of its location," said Holmes. "If they had they wouldn't have made the mistake they did."

"And what mistake was that?"

"Bexhill lies on the other side of Eastbourne and if they were going that way as they claimed then they could easily have given us the ride I asked for."

"Perhaps they don't like company," I added.

"That's a pity," said Holmes, "because we are going to visit them again."

"When?"

"Tonight, after dark. Perhaps they'll be more welcoming then."

Chapter Thirteen

Crane was still waiting for us though a little damp from the rain. "How did it go?" he asked, "I got a little worried. Were Randlett's thugs at the lighthouse?"

Holmes looked at him with some surprise. "Randlett? No. Dear me, this has nothing to do with Randlett. I'm afraid that your suspicions about your rival will not be confirmed upon this occasion."

I had thought as much. For all we had seen we had observed little of Randlett. As we climbed into Crane's vehicle and returned to Eastbourne I tried to order the facts in my mind just as Holmes had no doubt already ordered them in his. What did we know and where did the facts lead?

I tried to arrange the pieces of the puzzle so that they conjured up a picture, but try as I might I could not. The only real fact I knew was that two thugs had extracted money from Davis. Did they have other victims? If so who were they? What did the thugs know about them and why had no one called in the police authorities. I struggled with the picture for some time and then, admitting defeat, I turned to Holmes for enlightenment.

"It is a strange case. Crane saw everything but observed only what he wanted to believe, that a man called Randlett was conspiring in his downfall. I dare say you, Watson, might have given the matter of blackmail some thought, and yet if these thugs were mere blackmailers I think you'll have to admit they look pretty poor on it, eating beans and living in an abandoned lighthouse. There is no conspiracy and there is no blackmail, but there are, I am glad to say, plenty of clues."

Holmes was right. Neither conspiracy nor blackmail seemed to fit the bill but I couldn't bring to mind any of the clues that Holmes thought were in abundance. And yet, as Holmes was to point out, I had seen them all.

"First of all, we never witnessed any blackmail. Davis handed the money over without a qualm. He may well have owed the money quite legitimately to the men who came to his work."

That much was true. But if so, why did Crane's first printer disappear?

"Secondly, we know that the two men are strangers to Sussex. Why then did they choose to come here? What is it about this part of the world that attracts them?"

As I contemplated the matter Holmes took out his pipe, filled it with tobacco and lit it. The fog of London was once again upon us.

"Thirdly, didn't you find the fire unbearably hot even for a cold day like this. And why did it burn away so quickly, with not a stick of wood or coal in the place to refuel it?"

"The fire was not made to keep warm but to destroy something," I answered.

"Precisely. And if I am correct, the fuel came from the empty brown sacks we saw in the lighthouse."

I remembered that the same kind of sacks were to be found in *The Eastbourne Herald* printroom. What was it that Crane said they were used for?

"And," said Holmes, pausing to suck on his pipe, "what do you suppose were in those packages on the table?"

"I can't imagine," I said.

"Oh but you can, Watson. One printer abandons his post, another takes his place and this new printer is so fond of his work that he is prepared to hand over money to two villains without so much as a whimper. Why I have almost given it to you."

And indeed he had. The picture was now perfectly clear as was the reason for Holmes insistence on returning to the lighthouse. The adventure was not yet over and a long dark night lay ahead of us.

Chapter Fourteen

At ten o'clock that evening Holmes, Crane and myself were in the woods not twenty yards from the lighthouse. There was but a sliver of moon and by it we watched the two thugs leave the lighthouse and climb into their carriage. Within minutes they were over the crest and heading into Eastbourne. As soon as they were out of sight we ran to the lighthouse door. It was locked. Holmes reached into his pocket and brought out a small leather case, "I thought we might need this," he said and opened it to reveal a set of locksmith's tools and an array of skeleton keys. Within less than a minute he had opened the door and we were inside.

A candle was burning in one corner of the room. "Ah," said Holmes, "just as I had suspected. Our friends will be back within the hour and they'll be bringing company."

"Who?" asked Crane.

"Davis," said Holmes. "I'm afraid that Davis is your criminal not Randlett."

Crane started to splutter some reply but Holmes quietened him. Now was not the time for explanations. "Try to locate the packages we saw earlier. That's the evidence we need."

"Evidence for what?" asked Crane. Holmes had already begun searching the room, moving what little furniture there was. "Evidence of the crime," he said. "Mr. Davis your printer is not quite the assiduous employee you would like to think. His appearance at your door the moment Mr. Evans had been persuaded to leave was no coincidence."

"But he is being blackmailed, Mr. Holmes."

"If only it were that simple. How much did Mr. Davis hand over to his blackmailers?"

"Why, five-pounds?"

"A princely sum indeed," I added, "and far more than the man earns in a week I dare say."

"Well, yes, but ..."

"My friend Watson is not decrying your generosity, Mr. Crane. He is merely pointing out that it is unlikely that Davis could afford such a sum. So the question is, where did he get it?"

Crane was temporarily stumped for an answer. It had never occurred to him to ask how Davis was able to give the crooks a sum greater than that he earned. He thought about it while Holmes and I continued our search. The fire in the grate had gone out and the room was considerably colder than it had been earlier in the day. A frost was forming on the windows and our breath hung in the air like icy mist. I opened the oven door but found nothing but ash inside. Satisfied that there was nothing in the living quarters Crane picked up the candle and together we climbed the spiral staircase to the top of the lighthouse.

"A wonderful sea view, eh, Watson?" said Holmes as he pointed at the large windows that overlooked the ocean. "Perhaps we should come back during the day to get the full effect of the vista." Holmes was laughing as he made the remarks. The sea air may have done nothing for his health but skulking about in the darkness while solving a crime had certainly lightened his mood.

By the candle's meagre light we searched the upper floor. At the centre of the room stood the huge circular reflector that was used to cast the lamplight across the sea. It rested on a large wooden platform that housed a gearing mechanism and at the side of the platform were two maintenance doors. Holmes opened them and searched inside while I went to examine two large cupboards that lay against the rear wall. Crane held on to the candle and begged for further explanation.

"Will you gentlemen please tell me what you're looking for?" I was just about to tell him when Holmes shouted out, "Eureka!" and pulled a large brown package from beneath the reflector. He laid it on the floor and quickly undid the twine that held it together.

"Gentlemen, I must insist. What is going on?" said Crane.

Holmes looked up at him as he continued to unwrap the package. "Mr. Crane, this is where Davis got his money."

Crane knelt down and held the candle close as Holmes spread the paper open. "My God," said Crane, "I've never seen so much money." We were looking at a king's ransom in five-pound notes. Thousands of pounds worth, and none of them worth a penny.

"Every one of them is counterfeit," said Holmes, "Davis is indeed a skilled printer but he couldn't have done it without the use of your Miehle printing machine. That's why he and his cronies created the vacancy at your newspaper."

Crane was astonished at the discovery. "I had no idea," he said. "And what about Randlett? What part does he play in all this?"

Before Holmes could answer we heard the downstairs door open. "I think the game's up, gentlemen," whispered Holmes. He blew out the candle and asked Crane to stand by the wall. Holmes and I took up positions either side of the doorway, myself to the left and Holmes to the right near the window.

We heard the door open and men talking as they entered. They didn't seem to miss the candle they had left alight, and by the glow from the staircase we knew that they had simply lit another one in its place. We must have waited for at least half an hour in the darkness, saying nothing. I looked at the large windows and noticed a railed balcony outside. It seemed to be our only exit and I wondered whether we could jump to the ground in safety. Then I remembered the portly Crane and knew that was not an option.

Suddenly there was the sound of footsteps coming up the stairs and the glow from the candle grew brighter. Holmes motioned me back from the doorway. Reluctantly I withdrew the revolver from my pocket. After being in the darkness for so long the light from the candle was blinding as it came into the room and I could not see who held it. Holmes did though, or at least he saw enough to strike the holder a severe blow on the chin. The man fell back, dropping the candle to the floor where it rolled and flickered before finally going out. As the man moved across the window I could see that it was the taller of the two thugs. He wasted no time in recovering his composure, shouted to his associate for help and pulled a knife from his pocket.

Holmes too was silhouetted against the window, fists clenched and ready to strike again. "I would advise you to drop the knife," said Holmes, "my friend behind you has a gun and he's a very good shot."

The thug turned towards me and peered into the darkness. I waved the gun at him indicating that he should move towards the centre of the room. Instead he lunged towards me with the knife, cutting me across the hand. The gun dropped to the floor as he said, "You don't have a gun no more." He was about to dive to the floor for it when Holmes pulled him back, spun him around and delivered a second punch to his chin.

"What's happening?" The shorter man ran into the room followed by Davis. They had heard the scuffle and had come expecting trouble. Both had large pieces of wood in their hands to use as weapons.

"Look out! It's a trap. One of 'em is behind the door," shouted the tall man. Davis lashed out with his stick and I ducked just in time to avoid what would have been a devastating blow. The other man had already set about Holmes, but was no match for his boxing skills, and on the third punch he dropped to the floor like a sack of coal.

Davis had given up trying to find me in the shadows and I had given up on finding the gun. As he turned towards Holmes I leapt at him and rugby tackled him to the ground, but he was up before me and struck out with a kick. Fortunately I had the good sense to roll across the room out of the way and his boot only caught me a glancing blow across the chest.

Holmes was unassailable, his lightning fast reactions sending his opponents reeling. They appeared to have no other plan than to attack him one after the other until they grew tired. "This is certainly warm work," said Holmes. I could only see him in silhouette but nevertheless I was sure he was smiling. As I went to stand up and join the fray, light suddenly flooded into the room. It was followed by a gunshot, the roar of which nearly burst my eardrums. I feared that one of the thugs had found my revolver.

The light that now filled the room had the effect of freezing us to the spot. I could see the tall thug unconscious on the floor at Holmes's feet. The short man was on his knees nursing a bloody jaw and Davis clung tiredly to a length of wood, his face bruised by Holmes's well-aimed punches.

A fourth man stood by the door holding a lantern in one hand and a smoking gun in the other. To my surprise it was Randlett. I noticed too that it was not my gun he held. "You've arrived in the nick of time," said Holmes, "Davis here was taking quite a beating."

I wasn't sure it was the time for merriment and looked nervously at Holmes waiting for his signal to either acquiesce or fight on. To my astonishment Holmes did neither. Instead he walked across to Davis and casually took the stick from his hand. And as he took it several policemen emerged from the stairway behind Randlett, dragged the thugs up from the floor and handcuffed them and Davis together. One of the policemen, a sergeant, introduced himself.

"Mr. Holmes and Dr. Watson, if my information is correct. I'm very pleased to meet you."

"An unexpected but welcome pleasure," said Holmes, "you were too late for the party but are a welcome guest all the same."

"Did you summon the police, Holmes?" I asked.

"No I did," said Randlett, "I'm not putting good money into Eastbourne only to have it taken over by petty criminals. I've had all sorts of complaints about them from my shop owners and I've warned them twice to leave. When I saw them at the lighthouse this afternoon I knew it was time to take action. So I contacted the sergeant and here we are."

"At this hour?" I asked.

"Oh it's not an official visit," said Randlett, "we were just going to gently encourage them to leave if you know what I mean."

"I know what you mean," said Crane derisively.

"You may not applaud my methods, Mr. Crane, but I hope you found them timely. Perhaps you'll find something good to say about me in next week's paper."

We left Crane and Randlett to discuss their differences and showed the sergeant the package of counterfeit money we had discovered. His after-hours favour for Eastbourne's leading citizen, and as Holmes later explained to me, fellow freemason, had suddenly become official police business of the highest import. "There might even be a commendation in it," said Holmes and the sergeant began to polish his buttons at the very thought.

The following morning found us sitting once again at the end of the pier looking out towards the distant horizon. The weather had cooled considerably and we shivered in our coats. My ribs ached, my hand hurt and Holmes's swollen knuckles had drawn considerable comments from the locals, several of whom asked if he was the prize-fighter from the nearby fair. But despite our injuries we were both in a cheerful frame of mind and had spent the last few minutes reflecting on the events of the previous day.

"It was the five-pound note that first aroused my suspicions," said Holmes, rubbing his sore hands, "and I thought that the simplest way for a printer to arrive at such a considerable sum would be to print it himself. I wondered too why a man who prints black and white for a living would keep so many pots of coloured ink."

Holmes fumbled in his coat for his pipe, searching first in his right pocket and then in his left. Appearing to think better of it he came out empty handed and breathed in the sea air in lieu of his usual tobacco fumes.

"And what Crane thought was blackmail was merely Davis handing over a sample of his criminal work, a forged note," I said.

"Yes, printing such fine filigree as is found on Her Majesty's currency is notoriously difficult. There would have been many misprints. That is why he always insisted on taking away the waste paper," said Holmes. "That's what they were burning at Belle Tout lighthouse when we arrived."

"But what about the plates that Davis required to produce the notes? Where are they?" I asked.

"The sergeant asked me the same question. I told him to investigate a squeaking door in Crane's office. I suspect the plates are hidden in the panelling and the weight has forced the door to grind against its hinges."

Holmes rattled off the explanation as if the panelling of a door was a perfectly normal place to hide something you didn't want anyone to find. It made me wonder what Holmes had hidden in the doors of our Baker Street lodgings.

Holmes had a copy of *The Times* under his arm. He had glanced at it over breakfast and the contents reminded us that we both had unfinished business back in London. While we were fighting for our lives in the Belle Tout lighthouse, a young lady had lost hers in Mayfair. The murderer had struck again, five women were now dead, and despite Dr. Schermann's presence he still remained free to stalk the capital with impunity.

The tide had receded, leaving dark moist sand and shallow pools in its wake, and the gulls had descended to see what creatures they could find trapped within them. We had come to the end of another adventure and its success had buoyed our spirits. Our convalescence was over and it was time to travel to London with its dark buildings, grimy streets and poisonous fogs. It seemed to be another world and I was unsure that I wanted to return. It was while I contemplated such rebellious thoughts that Holmes spoke. He did not turn his head, but continued staring at the far horizon where the sea and sky seemed to be melting together under the hazy light of a rising sun.

"I've enjoyed our short break, Watson. I didn't think I was going to, but I did, and I'm very glad I came. It's a matter of perspective. When I first arrived I did not observe what was here and only noticed what was not. But the south coast certainly has its attractions and I can envisage returning, some day."

"For another holiday?" I asked. "Or maybe you'll retire here, Holmes. You could walk the promenade or sit and reminisce on the pier. I'm sure there'd be no shortage of listeners."

"Perhaps," said he, "but there's another reason that might draw me back."

"And what would that be?"

"To find my pipe. I seem to have lost it in the tussle at Belle Tout."

We laughed and then sat in silence for a few moments more as the sun's ascendance cast its warm rays on the cold retreating tide. At its height it gilded the grey clouds with a crimson glory and, even in the chill of the winter air, we could feel the heat of it on our upturned faces. That we would swap this divine sight for the squalor of London seemed insane. But London called and who could let that plaintive cry go unanswered?

Chapter Fifteen

We enjoyed the rest of the day in Eastbourne doing nothing in particular. A walk, some sightseeing, a meal: all were done at a leisurely pace and neither of us made any mention of what would happen upon our return to London. I felt, though, that the sun and fresh sea breezes, cold as they were, had somehow cleansed and prepared us for a new onslaught on an old foe. We took a late train back to London and watched the landscape grey as we approached the great city, fields and streams giving way to sprawling suburbs and the soot black wastelands of industry. The air grew thicker too and the train slowed to a crawl as it hit one of London's notorious pea-soupers, a miasma of fog and pollution that somehow we had all come to regard as a fair price to pay for living in the metropolis. We hailed a cab outside the station and were ferried in silence to our Baker Street lodgings.

We toasted our return with a late night brandy and then slept. I dreamt I was back in Eastbourne, sitting on a bench at the end of the pier and looking out to sea. A fog could be seen on the horizon and as I watched, it slowly crept in. I looked behind me and the tall white buildings that lined the shore seemed to be somehow nearer, pressing in on me, their windows staring like the eyes of blind men. The fog was now at the end of the pier, rolling onwards, a dark swirling cloud that seemed almost alive. From somewhere

97

within, I heard the sound of two people arguing. Then silence followed by a loud and agonising scream. I quickly turned to my friend Holmes and was astonished to find that he was no longer beside me. I sat numb with fear, blindly gazing into the mist and unable to shake off a feeling of utmost dread. Slowly, from out of the fog, a figure approached, its footsteps sounding hollow on the pier's wooden deck and growing louder with each step. I have no memory of what happened next, and for that I am most grateful.

Holmes was awake early the next morning, as was always the case when he had business of importance to attend to, and for Holmes there was no more business more important than that of an unsolved crime. He had already left Baker Street when I awoke and returned while I was taking breakfast, bringing with him a bundle of newspapers.

"I thought these might be useful," he said as he placed them on the table. I had expected the morning's *The Times* but instead was confronted by a collection of *The Sunday Referee* which extended back some weeks. He could see from my puzzled expression that I had no idea of what relevance *The Sunday Referee* was to our present case.

"Oh, I forgot to tell you that Mr. Sims will be joining us today. I sent him a telegram from Eastbourne," said Holmes.

I had forgotten about my conversation with Sims, but even so I had not imagined that Holmes would ever take him up on his invitation to be interviewed. I should have asked what purpose the meeting would serve, but to be truthful, having just awakened my mind was in no fit state to consider such matters. I was also a little slow in making the connection between the newspapers and George Sims, so Holmes explained while he poured himself a cup of Darjeeling.

"Sims writes a weekly column in *The Sunday Referee* under the name of Dagonet. I thought it would be wise to see what he has made of the Mayfair murders."

"I'm sorry, Holmes," I said, "It is early."

"Yes indeed, Watson, but Mr. Sims has already sent word that he will be with us at noon and we have a lot of reading to do." With that, he poured a little milk into his tea, stirred it and unfolded the first newspaper. I took the second, and one by one we worked our way through the pile, digesting Mr. Sims's words of wisdom along with the occasional slice of toast.

I've never trusted those who write under pseudonyms, not since I discovered that George Eliot was a woman. I was sure that Sims's adopted name of Dagonet was something infinitely clever, but I'm afraid it was beyond me, and I didn't want to appear foolish by asking Holmes to once again explain something which might turn out to be blindingly obvious. Instead I pressed on, reading each article and then exchanging it for the one Holmes had read. The only thing that was obvious to me was that Dagonet was awfully full of himself. No matter what the problem, whether political, technical or social, he claimed to have the answer without actually revealing what it was. What he did do was use his literary conjurations to cast aspersions on the work of the government, industry and any other social institution that did not come up to his lofty standards. His column was one of self-importance and mockery and each reading made the forthcoming meeting less pleasurable. Holmes, though, showed no sign of displeasure. He merely read, drank his tea and formed his opinions quietly.

The latest edition of *The Sunday Referee* contained yet another account of the manner in which Mr. Sims became a suspect in the notorious 'Jack the Ripper' case. It was a story he told often – every time there was a murder in London – and he embellished it with each telling. It happened at the height of the hysteria surrounding the 'Ripper' slayings, the night of 30th September 1888 to be precise. As Sims described it, a wild looking individual stopped by an evening coffee-stall for some refreshment. He chatted a little about the murders, but this was not unusual, as it was the sole topic of conversation at the time. The stall-keeper said that there would no doubt be another murder soon. The stranger agreed but added, "Perhaps you may hear of two tomorrow morning." The reply seemed a little too specific for idle talk and frightened the stall-keeper no end. It terrified him even more when he noticed fresh blood stains on the stranger's shirt cuffs. Fearful, he said nothing. The stranger smiled, finished his coffee and then left.

It wasn't until the following morning that the stall-keeper discovered that there had indeed been two murders that very night. Alarmed and excited he told everyone that he had come face to face with the 'Ripper'. He was on his way to inform the police when he saw the face of the 'Ripper' again. This time it was a photograph on the cover of a magazine. A photograph of George R. Sims. "That's the man. That's the 'Ripper'," said the stall-keeper, and he took the magazine and his story to the police. Of course it was all a mistake. Sims had an alibi and was never seriously under suspicion. Nevertheless it made an entertaining anecdote that Sims has used on many occasions.

When noon arrived so did George Sims, announcing his presence by rapping a heavy cane upon the door. I welcomed him in and Holmes had him take one of the armchairs by the fireplace. There was a momentary pause while we all settled. As I looked at Sims I could see why he might be mistaken for a murderer. He had small darting eyes that flicked to and fro like a lizard's. They looked out of a face that was largely hidden by a big black bushy beard. It looked like one of Holmes's theatrical disguises. His hair was dark and thick but combed close to his head like a carelessly woven carpet. He glanced about, waiting for one of us to speak. I could think of nothing particular to say to the man, other than I loathed his newspaper column, when I suddenly realised I had no idea as to why Holmes had invited Sims to visit. It was Holmes himself who broke the silence.

"Thank you for taking the trouble to visit on such a bitterly cold day, Mr. Sims. What can we do for you?"

"Well, can I be frank?" said Sims.

"Please do," replied Holmes; "honesty is a rare commodity these days."

"Well," said Sims, rather hesitant in spite of his promised frankness, "I wondered whether you had formed any opinion about the recent murders."

"And why should I?" said Holmes.

"Well," said Sims for the third time, "it is your trade, is it not, the detection of crime?"

Holmes steepled his fingers and leaned back in his chair before saying, "I am a consulting detective, Mr. Sims, and am presently working on a number of intriguing cases, but I have to be equally frank and say that I have not, as yet, been consulted on the matter of the Mayfair murders."

I could see that Sims was about to enquire further but Holmes continued after only the briefest of pauses.

"I think that you should visit my good friend Inspector Lestrade and the amazing Dr. Schermann. Perhaps they could help you with any enquiries you may have in that direction. In fact, now that I think of it, it would make an excellent article for your column.

An exclusive interview with Europe's latest detective sensation."

"Oh, I intend to," said Sims. "I have an appointment with the remarkable Doctor this very afternoon. I was most impressed with his demonstration at the British Museum last week."

I was about to intercede and tell Sims that he should beware of sensationalising Schermann's spurious claims when I saw Holmes give a glance in my direction. For some reason he wanted me to remain silent on the matter and with great reluctance I kept my counsel.

"Have you spoken with Dr. Schermann yet?" said Sims somewhat warily, "I'm sure you have much to discuss being fellow travellers as it were in the arts of detection."

"I'm afraid not. Our methods are very different and I do not share his interpretations of graphology."

"Oh, it was very impressive," said Sims. "Lady Bradford thought it one of the most exciting advances in criminal science she has ever witnessed. She is his patron, you know."

"Then I'm sure he will take note of her opinion."

"So might you, Mr. Holmes. She is after all married to the Commissioner of the Metropolitan Police."

"My tobacconist is married, but I would not ask his wife to recommend a good smoking pipe," said Holmes making his point somewhat sharply. Sims had no trouble detecting the annoyance in Holmes's voice and pressed on while he thought he had the advantage.

"If you had stayed a little longer, you would have witnessed the most extraordinary demonstrations. You have only to write your name and Dr. Schermann seems to know everything about you."

"He gave you a personal demonstration, I take it?"

"Oh yes. Most extraordinary. Just by looking at the loops and lines of my signature he gave me the most marvellous character reading. It was very accurate indeed."

I could see that Holmes was wearying of the conversation. He had no wish to hear just how 'extraordinary' or 'marvellous' the Doctor was. Nevertheless, the facts, no matter how unpalatable, needed to be known.

"Very interesting, Mr. Sims. And do you recall what the good Doctor made of your literary hand?"

"I do indeed. I wrote down every word." And with that he reached unprompted into his coat pocket and took out several folded sheets of paper. He opened them and without further ado began to read.

"This is the hand of a creative man. A careful thinker. He is a communicator who can change destinies with a few well-chosen words. This man is a leader with high moral values. A teacher who can bring knowledge to those who follow him. He gives without regard for reward and is apt to sacrifice his own needs for the necessities of others. Above all he has an enquiring mind and an ability to seek the light where others see only darkness."

He read it slowly and carefully, gauging our faces for reaction before bringing his oratory to a close. He held the papers out as if expecting applause.

"Very flattering," said Holmes, "you appear to have no faults. What a rare man you are and how perceptive of Dr. Schermann to spot it."

Sims, for all his faults, was by no means unaware of Holmes's disbelieving tones.

"I'm afraid you're wrong there, Holmes. Dr. Schermann said," and he began to read one final paragraph, "If he has one fault it is that he is kinder to others than himself. He is prepared to suffer for a cause he believes in and endure ridicule for his honest aspirations."

Sims looked at Holmes and myself as if he had just read from the Gospels. Holmes narrowed his eyes and thereby revealed his utter disbelief. I could see that he found the whole thing completely incredible. How had a man like Sims, blowhard though he was, been taken in so easily?

"As I say, very flattering, but somewhat subjective, I think you would agree. Who among us would not like to be talked about in those terms?"

"But who among us is?" answered Sims smiling. He folded the papers and slipped them back into his pocket. "The fact is that Scotland Yard have invited Dr. Schermann to help them rather than yourself. Is that not so, Holmes?"

Holmes did not answer. He rose from his chair, walked over to the mantelpiece and picked up his pipe. The action of filling it with tobacco seemed to calm his mood. "Well, I shall be most curious to see what you make of Dr. Schermann and how you present him to your readers."

"I shall send you a copy of the article the very moment it is printed," said Sims. He looked at his pocket watch and then stood as if to leave, saying, "By the way, do you have any thoughts as to who is committing these murders, Holmes?"

"Now isn't that a question you should be asking Dr. Schermann?"

"Oh, I will. I just thought ..."

"I wouldn't presume to trample on a fellow detective's case," said Holmes, "It would be most unprofessional, don't you agree?"

Sims had no time to reply. Holmes handed him his cane, shook his hand, ushered him to the door and bade him farewell. As Sims descended the stairs Holmes called after him with a rather overdone enthusiasm, "And I look forward to reading your article." Sims waved his cane in acknowledgement and then was gone.

Holmes lit his pipe and sat back in his chair. "What do you make of that?" I asked. "Has everyone taken leave of their senses? That graphology reading was no more impressive than that of a fairground palmist. It was all air and no substance."

"We all succumb to flattery, Watson. Sims is no different from the rest."

"I agree, but with Dr. Schermann's help Scotland Yard can no more hope to catch the murderer than a man can walk on the moon."

"On the contrary. I believe the murderer will be caught and that Dr. Schermann will play a leading role in his capture."

"But how?" I asked.

"Flattery, dear Watson, flattery."

Chapter Sixteen

The fog that hid London showed little sign of fading. It ebbed and flowed like the tide but it was never far away. It had been several days since Sims's visit to Baker Street, and I had pondered on its significance. Holmes had purposely invited the man over, but for what purpose I did not know. The answer, I thought, would be in Sims's article when it was published and so, when Sunday came and *The Sunday Referee* delivered as Sims had promised, I read it with some anticipation. As expected, within its lurid covers lay a lengthy article written by George Sims in his usual bombastic style. But this time instead of heaping praise upon himself he placed it squarely on the shoulders of Dr. Schermann, extolling the virtues of his so called scientific methods and predicting that with Schermann now an official consultant to Scotland Yard, the Mayfair murderer might count his days numbered. A side panel contained the sycophantic graphology text that Sims had read to us in our lodgings. No mention was made of Holmes. I wondered how he would feel, once the doyen of detectives and now seemingly forgotten. Suddenly, and to my utter surprise, the door to our apartment opened and a familiar voice called out.

"They say absence makes the heart grow fonder, Watson. We may have an opportunity to put that old adage to the test."

It was Holmes, and he had a copy of *The Sunday Referee* in his hand. He cast the paper onto the table.

"I thought you were still asleep," I said.

"Too much to do, Watson. There are long days ahead of us and you may count this as the first."

"I take it the article wasn't to your liking, Holmes."

"On the contrary. It was exactly as I hoped it would be. I couldn't have written it better myself, apart from the odd grammatical error and the elimination of clichés, but then I suppose a schoolboy could have done as well. And you would think that after spouting endlessly on the same topic for over a decade the man might have something new to say."

"But it's such rot. How can he expect a tin pot trickster like Schermann to catch a murderer? And he doesn't even mention you, Holmes."

"Now calm yourself, Watson. There's no need to get angry on my account."

"It's an affront, that's what it is. And Lestrade – how on earth can he let this happen?"

"I don't think he will, Watson."

I paused for a moment to let the full weight of Holmes's words sink in. He seemed entirely unruffled by Sims's article and not the least reproachful of Lestrade.

"Now are you ready to join me for breakfast? The walk will sharpen the appetite."

"But Mrs. Hudson has already made breakfast," I said. The aroma of smoked kippers and coffee had drifted upstairs and had settled in the room like some invisible appetiser.

"Yes, she has. Well observed, Watson. However, I've told her to give it to a couple of the 'Irregulars', just as soon as they get back from a little task I've set them."

I attempted to question him further but instead found my hat placed upon my head and my coat around my shoulders.

"Come on, we wouldn't want to be late. It's not polite to let our guest dine alone." And with that enigmatic reference I was pushed out of the room and was on my way to a breakfast appointment I never knew I had.

The walk certainly did sharpen the appetite and my wits along with it. The grey mist had turned to yellow fog, as if it was starting to moulder and rot, and crushed in on us like a cold dead hand. We could see but a few feet ahead and heard the clacking footsteps and hacking coughs of invisible passers-by. Occasionally a tradesman or merchant would emerge from the darkness like the legendary Flying Dutchman, grimly preceded by the hollow rattling sound of his carriage wheels and the dim light of his lantern. The fog had a most disorienting effect and I was quickly lost. Holmes, however, strode on, guided by an innate sense of direction and purpose that I had long admired.

I followed him breathlessly and once or twice tried to question him. But he bade me stay silent on the subject until our breakfast, which, he informed me, was to take place in a small eating house just off Wigmore Street.

"I see we are nearly there," he said. I on the other hand could see nothing, at least not at first. Then the street seemed to suddenly narrow and dark walls emerged from the fog as if the city were closing in on us. Somewhere ahead lights hovered in the mist. As we walked closer I realised they were lanterns belonging to half a dozen carriages parked in a courtyard. I still had no idea where we were. It was certainly not the Wigmore Street I knew.

"Here we are Watson," said Holmes. We were standing outside a large black oak door. It was the only part of the building I could see. The door had a small thick glass window at its centre and somewhere behind it a fire glowed. "A couple of hard raps might gain us entrance," said Holmes. I knocked on the door several times then waited. A shadow crossed the window and then I heard a bolt being slid, and a few moments later the door opened slowly, as if it took considerable strength to pull. Holmes walked quickly inside. I stood there for a moment wondering where Holmes had taken us and then a voice called me in. "Don't dally, Watson; there's a warm fire within and a good breakfast to be had."

If there is an alternative map of London then Holmes is the man to draw it. I doubt it would be stocked at Stanford's, though. It would not be the prettiest of maps nor of any use to tourists, for no reasonable person would ever consider visiting the places it depicted. It would chart every seedy nook and cranny, every dark corner and neglected avenue; the spaces between the places we know and those we could never imagine. Holmes would make the ideal cartographer of the unknown, labelling its narrow maze of streets in the same way that the ancient mariners appended the warning, 'Here be monsters'.

This building was no exception for as I looked ahead I saw a cyclops, a one-eye giant standing before me. His right eye sparkled in the firelight but his left eye was but a fleshy fold, scarred shut after some monstrous accident. It reminded me of the terrible wounds I had witnessed in Afghanistan. The giant, I call him that for he was easily six and a half feet tall, seemed unaffected by my staring. He simply smiled and gestured for me to enter.

"Come now," said Holmes, "and shut the door behind you before the fog has us all." Then he turned to the one-eyed man and introduced us. "Joshua, this is my colleague, Dr. Watson. A gentle voice whispered forth, a voice that belied the man's tough appearance and horrific scar. "Pleased to meet you, Dr. Watson. Very pleased indeed."

Then he turned to Holmes and said, "I've saved the table in the corner for you, Mr. Holmes. I hope it's to your liking." As we took our seats I said, "You have unusual friends, Holmes."

"Well you should know, Watson. You're one of them!"

I soon learned that Joshua had indeed acquired his injury in battle, an unwelcome souvenir of the Afghan war. Upon leaving the army he bought himself this hideaway, catering to the needs of those who work the nocturnal hours, deliverymen, cabbies and even the police. More than that, it was a halfway house between respectability and illegality, where a bobby and a burglar might sup side by side, temporarily forgetting their differences as information was exchanged for a few shillings. It is a place where informants might ply their trade without fear of arrest. I wondered whom our guest would be and what he had to tell.

"This is a fine place you've brought me to," said I.

"It is indeed," said Holmes, deliberately missing my point. He nodded in the direction of an elderly man sitting in the corner, noisily eating a bowl of soup. He appeared to be overly dressed even for this harsh weather, as if he carried the stock of an entire clothes shop on his back and tied it in place with numerous scarves. "That," said Holmes, "is 'Billy Three Coats'."

"I should say he's wearing more than three."

"I'm sure you're right. But despite his eccentricities he's a good man, a second generation cabbie who knows London even better than I."

'Billy Three Coats' nodded back to us and gave us a toothless smile.

"And to his right you'll see 'Sweet Apple Joe' and 'Tommy Tin Whistle'."

The two men were drinking ale and playing cards. I didn't need Holmes's powers of deduction to see where Tommy had derived his name, the tin whistle was sticking out of his top pocket and I assumed he used it to keep himself amused during some passengerless hours. If the stack of pennies by his side was anything to go by, he seemed to be the luckier, or more skilful, of the two players. As for the other man, 'Sweet Apple Joe', I had no idea from where his moniker might have originated. He was a strong looking stocky character with a head like a rock and hands like hams. He looked far from sweet.

"And how did 'Sweet Apple Joe' come by his name?" I asked.

"By complete accident, and I'm glad to say that the jury concurred."

"Jury?"

"Yes, Joe used to be a porter at Covent Garden market."

"Oh, and he sold sweet apples there?"

"Not at all. As I say, he was a porter, he sold nothing, but carried whatever he was paid for. It so happens that he was carrying a barrel of sweet apples when he came upon a robbery in the market. They say he threw the barrel over twenty feet – some say thirty but I think they exaggerate, you know how these stories are – and it struck both robbers killing them instantaneously. The jury came to the conclusion that it was death by misadventure, but how they came to that decision is not a point that is dwelled upon."

I dare say it wasn't. One look from the man across the courtroom would be enough to convince anyone that a decision about his fate should not be taken lightly. 'Sweet Apple Joe' was indeed a powerful looking figure who seemed to have been put together from stone and clay and one would go to great lengths to avoid causing him any annoyance.

Several other people sat around the darkly furnished room and Holmes could name them all.

A roaring fire made the rough dark oak gleam like jet and cast wavering shadows across its curious inhabitants. They were all cabmen, breakfasting after a long night's work or preparing themselves for a hard day ahead, still wrapped in their winter coats and scarves, their hats by their plates. Except for a nod or two of recognition, they ignored our presence completely, being too busy consuming their meals before returning home or to the streets in hope of picking up a fare or two. I didn't fancy their chances of making much money today. The fog had cleared the streets. It was not a day for travelling.

Joshua came to the table and Holmes ordered two breakfasts. I meant to ask him what exactly a breakfast here might consist of but I thought better of it. I was beginning to miss the kippers that even now were cooking in Mrs. Hudson's kitchen. Two mugs of coffee arrived and I was just about to press Holmes for further details when the door opened and a man walked in, coughing, the fog at his back. He closed the door quickly and then glanced about the room as if looking for someone. He wore a long dark coat and a brown muffler across the lower half of his face. I was about to ask Holmes who he was when he looked directly at us and started to walk towards our table.

"A friend of yours?" I whispered.

"A friend of us both," answered Holmes.

The man pulled up a chair and sat down. He looked very familiar

"I see you got my message," said Holmes to the stranger.

"What message was that?" I asked.

"One of Holmes's scurvy helpers. Thomas, wasn't it?" answered the stranger from behind his muffler. It was a voice I knew but couldn't place.

"That's right, Thomas. A good lad, probably enjoying a kipper breakfast about now. I said meet me here if you have something to tell. I take it you have."

"Holmes, please be discreet. This could mean my job. My career."

Now I recognised our mysterious guest's voice. It was none other than Inspector Lestrade! That he had come here to this strange place was a sign that he had much to tell indeed.

"Have no fear," said Holmes, "We're here to help each other. I have many questions, but a man can't answer on an empty stomach. So let's eat first and talk later." And with that he summoned over the Joshua and asked him to bring an extra breakfast.

"Of course, Mr. Holmes," whispered the giant, "And what about a hot cup of coffee, Inspector Lestrade?"

Lestrade flushed. He pulled the muffler aside and gave out a sigh. "Yes, Joshua. Coffee too. It seems I don't have your knack for disguise Mr. Holmes." He was tired, his features haggard and his eyes weary.

"It takes more than a scarf, Lestrade. Next time you might try some false whiskers or a pair of spectacles. I have some you can borrow."

Lestrade laughed. "I'm sure you do, Holmes. Now that my poor charade is over I can at least enjoy breakfast. Isn't that what a condemned man has, a hearty breakfast? I've been on watch all night, am frozen to the marrow and as hungry as a dog."

"Then you'd better bring that coffee quickly, Joshua, Lestrade has much to tell us and a hot drink will loosen his tongue wonderfully."

113

And so it was, in this extraordinary place, in the midst of fog-laden London and watched over by a cyclopean giant, Inspector Lestrade became our reluctant informant.

Chapter Seventeen

I thought the breakfast greasy but my two companions did not seem to notice and, taking their silence as approval, I decided not to remark upon it. We were barely half way through our meal when Holmes asked the Inspector to lay his cards upon the table. What information were they holding at Scotland Yard that had not been made public? Lestrade looked up from his plate and began to list the sorry details of the affair, gesturing with his knife as if to underline the important points.

"Five women, none known to the other, murdered in Mayfair. All strangled. The times and places you know. There is no obvious motive. One common factor is that all the women were relatively new to London and had little time to make any acquaintances."

"No gentleman friends, I take it," I said.

"Only one, and she was engaged. No dark pasts, nothing to haunt them, nothing to run away from. They came to London to better themselves, that is all. It is a pity the city did not treat them well."

Holmes appeared unmoved as if there were nothing extraordinary about five unsolved murders. "Come, come," he said, "that much we can read in the papers. There's something else, Lestrade. Out with it, man. You came here to tell me something and now you can't find the words."

Lestrade remained silent as if a heavy weight lay upon his conscience. "That is quite another matter," he said, "it is Dr. Schermann I came to discuss."

"Schermann can wait. There is something about these murders that you are holding back from the newspapers, isn't there? A little detail that you hope might give away the murderer at some future point. I'll wager you have a description of our killer, don't you?"

Lestrade looked back at his plate and began to carve up a fatty sausage that lay there. Holmes knew the look of a man with something to hide and pressed forward his advantage.

"There is! I'm right. And I'll astonish you further because I can tell you what that detail is. You just have to nod your head, or wave your knife, Lestrade. I wouldn't want it said that one of Scotland Yard's leading officers was party to giving away confidential information."

"Then for heaven's sake say it quietly, Holmes. There are many ears wagging."

"Oh, don't worry. No one here is likely to tell a tale. Not for free anyway."

I had no idea what Holmes was about to say to Lestrade. I remembered the clippings from the newspapers pasted all over the walls at our Baker Street lodgings, but had no inkling that he had made any deduction from them. Holmes leant across the table and uttered a phrase that nearly made the Inspector choke on his breakfast.

"You believe the murderer is a woman!"

Lestrade spluttered in surprise and began a coughing fit that drew the eyes of everyone in the room. It came to an end when Joshua struck him a hefty blow on the back. "Something stuck in my throat," said Lestrade by way of explanation. Joshua nodded and then went away. Everyone else returned to minding their own business.

"How could you know?" asked Lestrade.

"I know your methods," said Holmes, "I have no doubt that you have several witnesses to the young ladies' final hours. You surmised, quite rightly, that they must have known their killer for them to be taken so utterly by surprise.

Most killers are men and you expected witnesses to give you a description that fitted that common profile. Unfortunately none of them did. In fact to your amazement they all recalled last seeing the victims in the company of a woman ... the same woman. That is the fact you have been hiding from the newspapers. That is the fact you expect to lead you to the assassin."

"Absolutely right. The same woman each time."

"And how was she dressed?" asked Holmes.

"Finely by all accounts. An olive green skirt and jacket over a white frilled blouse embroidered on the collar. She wore a fashionable hat with a veil; naturally this has hindered any facial description. The hat matched her clothes in colour and I believe it sported a feather, the nature of which is in some dispute. Oh, and she had a fur stole and gloves. There is no doubt about it. It was the same woman every time ... a murderess in Mayfair. Who would have believed it?"

Lestrade looked relieved to have told Holmes the facts but I could see that something else played on his mind. Holmes saw it too. "Let me put you out of your misery," said my friend. "There is one more facet to this case."

"Indeed there is, and you may as well know that too."

"I think I already do," said Holmes. "The question that needs to be asked is how the victims came to meet their murderer. And the answer is very simple. They advertised for her."

The clippings on the walls at Baker Street began to make sense. Holmes had been scouring the personal columns in search of clues and once again he had found them. "So that's what you were doing," I said, "I saw that the wall ..." I suddenly realised that I had not told Holmes of my visit to his room. I'm sure he noticed my slip but he chose to overlook it.

"Yes, I apologise if my behaviour seemed erratic but it was as efficient a way as any of examining the text for clues."

"And I take it you found them."

"Only one, but one was enough to suggest the rest. Perhaps the Inspector can confirm my suspicions. The women were new to London and they did what many lonely people in the metropolis have done before them. They advertised for friends. At least the first victim did, Miss Jane Little – only she used an anagram of her name, Jean Tillett I believe, to avoid embarrassment. I take it the other ladies also advertised under pseudonyms."

"That they did. When we searched their homes we discovered that all five had replies from the same woman. They were obviously replies to advertisements and it wasn't long before we were able to determine that they were placed in *The Times*. With some help from the advertising manager we confirmed that each victim had indeed placed notices in the agony column. Five different names were used on the replies but we are convinced they were written by the same hand."

"The correspondent didn't leave an address, I take it?"

"No. She met each of her victims at a different place at an appointed time. The first time was also the last."

"Has Dr. Schermann seen any of the handwritten notes yet?"

"Yes, he has subjected it to his psycho-graphology, but I certainly don't intend to make it public. I didn't mean to be abrupt with you the last time we met Holmes, but I tell you now so there is no misunderstanding, I have no faith in Dr. Schermann, but unfortunately my superiors think otherwise. The witness statements are a different matter. It is to our advantage to know that we are looking for a woman and not a man. I already have a sack full of confessions from every crackpot in London. I don't need any more. Most of them are from men. The few we have from women, we look into, naturally."

Inspector Lestrade hadn't intended to say so much but I could see that he felt the better for it. He picked up his knife and fork and continued his breakfast. Holmes looked pleased to have his suspicions confirmed. "And how did Dr. Karl Schermann come to be so closely involved with Scotland Yard," he asked.

"Ah that is a story Holmes. The man is a snake. He charms the birds from the trees and then devours them."

118

Lestrade forked a slice of sausage into his mouth by way of punctuation. He chewed, swallowed and then continued his tale, this time stabbing the air with his knife at every mention of Schermann's name. "No man likes to be made a fool of, least of all me, but I tell you that the only job I'll be fit for soon is clowning in Sanger's circus." He cut himself another slice of sausage. He was certainly as hungry as he claimed, putting away one bite after another with amazing rapidity.

"It's all Lady Bradford's fault. I don't blame Sir Edward. What's a man to do when a wife gets an idea into her head?" He continued to feed himself, and Holmes, getting a little impatient with the breaks in the story, prompted him to continue. Lestrade took a sip of coffee, laid his cutlery aside and told his tale without further distraction.

"I imagine it began in Paris. Sir Edward Bradford and his wife were there on an official engagement, guests of the French Police. Well, Schermann had already practised his witchery on the Parisians and they awarded him a medal for his trouble."

"What exactly did he tell them?" I asked.

"Same as he tells everyone else, I don't doubt, exactly whatever it is they want to hear!"

"And that I presume is what he told Lady Bradford," said Holmes.

"That's what I heard," replied Lestrade. "He used his psycho-graphology and read all manner of wonderful things in her handwriting. She is delighted and invites him to London before her husband can find the French for 'no'. And before you know it he's at Scotland Yard helping with our enquiries so to speak."

"And what has he managed to come up with?" asked Holmes.

"This," said Lestrade. He reached into his pocket, pulled something out and held it up for us to see. It was a length of chain on the end of which was fastened a latchkey.

Holmes and I sat there perplexed. This time Lestrade did not need further prompting. Our baffled looks were enough.

119

"It is a psychic pendulum, gentlemen. You hold it like so and it reveals the whereabouts of the criminal. I don't know why we never thought of it before!"

Lestrade held the apparatus above the table so that the key dangled from the chain. It moved back and forward as he spoke.

"Yes, gentlemen. We are being encouraged to carry these little devices about our person along with our lanterns and truncheons. When the criminal is nearby the key will swing to and fro like this. Why, look here, it's swinging already. Perhaps the murderer is in this very room!"

He threw the key onto the table and sat back, his face a picture of utter humiliation. I felt extremely sad for him and angry at Dr. Schermann that such superstition could find itself at the heart of our police force.

"These are desperate times," said Holmes, "and people are driven to desperate measures. The police investigation into the 'Ripper' was perceived as a failure. Now old superstitions are replacing science, especially when the charismatic Dr. Schermann peddles them to gullible women and they to their obliging husbands." He picked the key and chain from the table and examined them. "When will this psychic pendulum come into operation?"

"On the 6th February when Lady Bradford is holding a dinner in his honour, and he intends to unveil the pendulum then."

"Does anyone else know about this?"

"It's no secret. The press will be invited, led, of course by George Sims. He and Lady Bradford believe in Dr. Schermann and his pendulum wholeheartedly."

"Then we don't have much time. With your permission I would like to give the dubious doctor some additional publicity. You'll have to trust me, I'm afraid."

"What choice do I have? It's you or the pendulum," said Lestrade resigning himself to the less humiliating of the two alternatives. He took up his knife and fork and began to pick at his food. Holmes called over Joshua and ordered some more coffee.

"I wish you had come to me earlier," said Lestrade.

"That's one for the book," said Holmes to me, "I hope you are noting this down for *The Strand*, Watson."

"We could have avoided all this. We could have helped each other, Mr. Holmes. If I had allowed you in on our investigations then, perhaps together, we could have made some progress. I dare say the murdereress would be behind bars by now, eh Holmes?"

"I doubt it very much. This is no raging lunatic, no seeker of notoriety. The murderer is quiet, determined and methodical, and yet a slave to some insane compulsion, to kill and keep on killing until they are caught. And mark my words the murderer will be caught. The sooner the better for all of us."

"Do you have any idea who it could be?" asked Lestrade plaintively.

"None at all. But there is one thing we do know about the murderer."

"And what is that?" I asked.

"The murderer reads the newspapers, Watson."

"But I don't see how that helps us."

"Simple, Watson, the newspapers are the murderer's hunting ground and that is where we will lay our trap. Come, we have much to do. Thank you, Lestrade, you've been a great help and I hope to return the favour soon."

We left Lestrade to finish his breakfast, which was the least we could do, and set out into the fog and the unknown. The game was indeed afoot.

Chapter Eighteen

By the afternoon the fog had cleared a little and we took a hansom to George Sims's home, an opulent house in Conduit Street. A carriage was parked outside, the driver feeding the horse some oats from a bag. It was clear that we were not Sims's only visitors. We rang the bell and a well-dressed butler opened the door and led us to the library. "Mr Sims will be along in a moment, sirs. I trust you can make yourselves comfortable." A fire burned in an elaborate fireplace over which hung a large portrait. It took me a few moments to realise that the imposing figure depicted in the picture was George Sims. He wore a military uniform of some description, though I do not recall that he served in Her Majesty's Army, and struck a heroic pose. It was as accurate a reflection as might be found in a carnival mirror only instead of mocking its subject this one flattered it. The result, however, was the same, one of comic posturing. The butler added a few coals to the fire, bowing before the portrait of his master as if in supplication. Then he excused himself and left to attend his other duties. I sat myself in a leather armchair under the watchful gaze of Sims's image while Holmes, not a man to idle and filled with boundless curiosity, examined the books upon the shelves.

The library was well appointed, with a large window looking out upon the garden. The fog outside had dissolved into a fine haze, clear enough to see that at this time of the year the garden offered nothing more than a few bare trees and several evergreen borders to gaze upon. A small summer house gazed forlornly in my direction, abandoned during the winter months and looking eagerly to the spring, when, I imagine, the garden presented a much more pleasing picture. By the window stood Sims's writing desk, large and impressive and decorated with elaborate gilded scrollwork around its edges. It reflected the pomposity of the man; all bluff and bluster, a block of wood pretending to be gold. I felt pleased with my simile and was about to recount it to Holmes when Sims himself walked into the room.

"I'm sorry to have kept you," he said, "but I had another visitor, perhaps you saw her carriage outside."

"Yes we did," said Holmes, "Lady Bradford, was it not?"

"Yes indeed, your powers of deduction do you credit, Mr. Holmes."

"It was no power, Mr. Sims. We merely enquired of the driver outside. Why use logic when common-sense will suffice?"

I was unsure that Holmes's sharpness offered a prelude to good conversation but the remark did not seem to register with Sims who took his seat behind his desk and continued to talk about his aristocratic visitor.

"A most perceptive woman, Lady Bradford. She was thrilled by my article in *The Sunday Referee*. It was she who brought Dr. Schermann to the attention of Scotland Yard, you know. She intends to honour him at private function and I'm pleased to say that I have been invited."

"How interesting. It is Dr. Schermann we have come about," said Holmes getting right to the matter. He took a chair and steeled himself for the next part of his plan.

"Tell me frankly, Sims, do you think Dr. Schermann can catch this killer?"

Sims sat back in his chair, pleased to be asked his advice by the great Sherlock Holmes. As a look of smug self confidence came over him the resemblance to his portrait grew a shade closer.

"I most certainly do. He has the genius of Lombroso and Bertillon and has a new device to aid in the detection of crime."

"You mean the pendulum?"

Sims's eyes widened at the word. He was clearly surprised that Holmes knew of it. He opened a box of cigarettes that stood upon his desk and offered them around. We both declined.

"I hope you won't mind if I do," he said and proceeded to take one and light it. I believe they were French. A gift from Paris perhaps? Sims was soon wreathed in aromatic smoke.

"Have you seen the device, Mr. Holmes?"

"No but I have been told of its remarkable properties."

"Then perhaps I can enlighten you." Sims reached into his desk drawer, took something out. He held it up for us to see, admiring it as if it were a fine jewel. "This, gentlemen, is the apparatus that will revolutionise the art of criminal detection."

It was, as far as I could see, a large crystal pendant suspended from a chain. Sims dangled it over the table, the crystal swinging to and fro.

"And how does it work?" asked Holmes.

"Very simply, that is the beauty of it. As Dr. Schermann explains it, many of us know the answers to our problems but they are either buried deep within the subconscious or we are afraid to admit them. The pendulum magnifies our intuition and makes it visible. It guides our decisions and hones our choices. It is a compass through a sea of uncertainty. Unaffected by character or emotion it allows the user to learn the truth about what he thinks. That is the great benefit of the pendulum."

"But how would that specifically help in solving a crime?" I asked.

Sims laid his cigarette aside and then took some objects from his desk and arranged them out in a row. There were a pencil, a dictionary, a small brass paperweight and a photograph of a lady I took to be his wife. He held the pendulum over them and slowly moved it back and forth along the line.

"A demonstration then," he said. "I ask the pendulum a question. 'Who or what is dearest to my heart?' and I hold it so. I like my pencil; it is the tool of my trade, as is my dictionary. The paperweight is of no consequence, but the photograph – ah! that is a different matter."

As he spoke the crystal on the end of the chain started to move in a peculiar circular motion but only when he held it above the photograph. He moved it away and held it over the pencil and the crystal promptly halted its gyrations. Then he moved it back over the photograph and once again it started to circle as if impelled by some magnetic force.

"You see, gentlemen, the subconscious made visible. I assure you this is happening without any conscious movement on my part. The crystal does not tell lies, it reveals the inner secrets of a man's thoughts."

I tried to interrupt his literary speech but he had more to impart and held out a hand to stop me.

"No need to say it, Dr. Watson. You are still wondering what use this might be. Think of it this way. Our police are not fools but sometimes their emotions get the better of them and they take the wrong action or make the wrong choice. They arrest the innocent and let the guilty go free. Now, thanks to Dr. Schermann, our officers need only hold the pendulum above the photographs of the suspects and the truth of a situation will manifest itself. And when that suspect is brought to book, well then, it is they who hold the pendulum. Its movements will give away every lie. It is like reading a man's mind."

It sounded quite absurd and I found it difficult to believe that this foolishness had managed to infect a newspaperman like Sims, regardless of what I thought of his manner. He offered the pendulum to Holmes for his examination. He took out his glass as if making a thorough assessment but I could tell that he was merely indulging in play in order to gain Sims's confidence.

126

"And will you be informing your readers of this new device?"

"I will indeed. May I quote you, Mr. Holmes? *The Times* has decided to publish my article tomorrow."

"Quote me? Well, I had never thought of such a thing. Do you think anyone will care what I say? Surely Dr. Schermann is the man of the moment?"

"No, no, we may have our differences, Holmes, but London likes its home-grown heroes. I would very much like to quote you – if you have something particular to say, that is."

"I do indeed, but let me think on it a while and I will send it to you by messenger later today. Would that suit you?"

"Yes, absolutely. Don't make it too late now. The presses halt for no man."

"I'll send it over within the hour. It's been very informative, Mr. Sims, but I'm afraid we have to leave. Dr. Watson has an appointment he needs to keep."

It was the first I had heard of such a thing, but my day seemed to be filled with appointments I had not made. We shook hands and then Sims rang a bell for his servant, who showed us to the door.

We hailed a hansom and as it approached I asked Holmes what he made of Dr. Schermann's mysterious device.

"No time to discuss it now, Watson. We have your appointment." He took out his pocket watch and checked the time.

"And where would that be?"

"To meet a man who knows more about the occult and superstition than Madame Blavatsky herself."

"And who would that be?"

"Jacob Stone."

"And where would he be?" I said, exasperated that I was no nearer an answer.

"Why, where our adventure began – at the British Museum, of course."

Our adventure moved in circles, just like Schermann's pendulum, but where was it all leading? The pieces of the puzzle never quite fitted together in my mind and I had the feeling that Holmes still knew more than he had told. We stopped briefly at Baker Street where Holmes penned a note and then asked Thomas to deliver it. A short time later we were in Great Russell Street and walking once again through the portals of the British Museum. But this time, instead of mystification we would seek enlightenment and from a man I had never heard of but would surely never forget, the eccentric Jacob Stone.

Chapter Nineteen

Nestled at the heart of the British Museum is the reading room. It is in essence a huge dome set within a courtyard. High windows allow the sun to shine down on the scholars and academics who sit there quietly at the long reading tables that radiate out from its centre like the spokes of a huge wheel. In the summer it can be uncomfortably hot and in the winter it is equally cold. The sun hadn't shone on London for many days and when we entered the library that afternoon it bore an air of chilled gloom. We walked to the sound of our own footsteps and the occasional rustle of paper as a page was turned. Holmes led the way, approaching the librarian's desk in the middle of the room where an elderly man could be seen arranging a stack of books. He turned as he heard our approach and I recognised him as the librarian who had participated in Dr. Schermann's demonstration.

"Why, Mr. Holmes," he whispered. "What a surprise to see you. Do you require something? I don't recall you requesting any materials today."

"No indeed, Edward. That's not why I am here. By the way, may I introduce my esteemed colleague Dr. Watson. And this, Watson, is Edward Stevenson, librarian extraordinaire and compiler of the world's greatest catalogue of books, which currently stands at two thousand four hundred volumes, I believe."

"Two thousand five hundred, Mr. Holmes."

"I stand corrected. It is a prodigious collection, that much cannot be doubted."

Mr. Stevenson nodded appreciatively at Holmes's remarks. He was the very picture of a librarian, his greying hair unkempt, his thin spectacles poised on the bridge of his nose, his eyes looming large behind them. His eyebrows seemed to be permanently arched in surprise and his broad smile told of a man happy in his work.

"Then if you do not come to read, how can I help you?" said Stevenson.

"I'm looking for Jacob," said Holmes. "Do you know where he might be found?"

"Yes indeed. I saw him but an hour ago. He is busy at the racks, studying some taboo topic or another, as usual. Here, you'll need my key. You can leave it at the desk when you have finished."

Stevenson reached into his pocket and produced a thick bronze key and handed it to Holmes. Holmes thanked him and we walked to the back of the reading room until we could proceed no further. The walls are lined with high shelves, packed closely with books. Those that stood before us looked no different to the rest until I saw a keyhole set in one of the wooden uprights. Holmes inserted the key that Stevenson had loaned him. He twisted it twice and then pushed at the books. An enormous secret door swung open as the shelves and the volumes it contained turned on some delicately balanced hinge.

"Even this great library has its secrets," said Holmes as we walked through into another room. This room contained an array of glass cases beneath which lay a selection of rare illuminated manuscripts. We walked straight ahead and Holmes used the key to open another door, this one disguised as a wooden panel in the wall. Beyond that was a maze of narrow twisting corridors filled with large bound volumes containing newspapers from all over Britain. They were stacked one on top of the other, filling the corridors on either side until there was only the narrowest of spaces to walk through. There was little light and I stumbled frequently, my shins catching against the protruding volumes.

"My apologies for the awkwardness of our journey, Watson, said Holmes, "but the library is overrun with newspapers. They've been collecting them since 1820 and they've got rather more than they anticipated."

"They can't collect them forever."

"Others have said the same but the British Museum takes the opposite view and I'm afraid that I agree with them. All information is valuable, Watson, you know that. These newspapers have been gathered from all over the country; they form an immediate and as important a record of our history as anything to be found in books. Who knows what treasures our historians of the future may discover in their pages?"

He was right, but I couldn't help but wonder where such an immense archive could be stored. As the stacked volumes grew higher so they grew less tidy and our path became more difficult. Then, there was quite literally, light at the end of our tunnel. I could see an open door and a brightly lit room ahead of us. Suddenly the crowded corridor ended and a high-ceilinged room began, its walls lined with more books, ancient volumes and yellowing manuscripts. A great leaded skylight cast down coloured shafts of light in which dust motes flew. It lent the room an ochre tinge as if it had been pickled in formaldehyde. One entire wall contained beribboned scrolls projecting in great numbers from wooden racks, like the cannon of an ancient galleon. Another held faded texts imprisoned behind locked glass cabinets. The room was, to my eyes, in some disorder, as if someone had pulled books out from every shelf in search of one particular volume and had forgotten to put them back. They were upside down or spines inward or simply lay across one another horizontally as if the room had been shaken and the books had simply tumbled into their present positions. It was, in no uncertain terms, chaos.

At the centre of the room was a great four-sided tower of shelves filled with books in the same erratic fashion. A long ladder stood against each side of the tower and at the top of one of them, caught in a ray of amber light, was a curiously dressed man in a frock coat of some long out-moded fashion. He wore a stovepipe hat upon his head and he was replacing one of the volumes on the uppermost shelf. The shelf was just out of reach so he threw the book into position. It was a fortunate throw and the book stayed where it was put, overhanging the shelf by a third of its length. We did not call the book-thrower for fear of frightening him from his ladder but as it turned out we need not have been so cautious. Sensing our presence he cried out in a loud voice, "Visitors!" Without further ado he placed a foot at either side of his ladder and quickly slid all the way down, turning dust motes in his wake. As soon as his feet hit *terra firma* a cloud of dust erupted from the floor and the book he had just placed on the shelf fell down beside him, narrowly missing his head. He ignored it, spun himself around, stepped forward and held out his hand, saying, "Holmes! What brings you to my little abode?" It all happened with such speed that I for one was speechless.

The sprightly librarian had a large pale face and sharp features that made him look as if he had been chiselled from a block of alabaster. His hat was festooned with catalogue notes, held in place by pins, and amongst them was a grocery list on which potatoes, carrots and lamb were prominent. I suppose it was as convenient a place as any to keep his memoranda. It would certainly prevent them from being swallowed by the confusion that surrounded him. Beneath the hat a dark curl of hair poked out and lay upon his brow like an inverted question mark. He reminded me very much of Tenniel's illustration of the 'Mad Hatter'.

Holmes shook the man's hand and then introduced me. "Watson, meet Jacob Stone, keeper of the forbidden books."

"Glad to meet you," I said, adding, "Forbidden? Forbidden by whom?"

"Oh, just about everyone," said Jacob Stone, patting the dust from his frockcoat. "It's a censorious age, but then, when hasn't it been? Fortunately we collect the scorned, banned, proscribed and outlawed with the same passion as a cleric collects his hymnbooks at the end of a service. Good thing too. What is banned in one age often becomes custom in another. But enough talk! What can I do for you two gentlemen?"

Holmes explained our dilemma with particular reference to the pendulum that Dr. Schermann was to demonstrate. "I believe it's a device connected with the occult and I thought if there was one man alive who knew of it, it was your good self."

"Quite right, quite right. All our occult materials are here," said Stone. He led us both to a stack of shelves full to the brim with texts on witchcraft, alchemy, demonology and other supernatural matters. Once again I could make no sense of their order. Stone stopped in front of them, closed his eyes and then placed his fingers to his temples.

"A pendulum, you say. Well, I can certainly help you there. Now let me think."

His long fingers rubbed at his temples and he closed his eyes more tightly. His head nodded, his eyelids fluttered and his lips trembled as if reciting some great liturgy. The grocery list flapped back and forth on his hat. Holmes nudged me and said quietly, "Jacob is an eidetic. He remembers everything as if it were a photograph. That's why the books here are arranged in no particular order. He simply remembers where he last saw it."

"Amazing," I said though in truth I did not quite believe that anyone could produce order from the disarray I saw around us. Slowly Jacob Stone's mutterings grew louder and I could now hear that he was calling out a list of books; "*Malleus Malificarum, Medicina Magica, Demonic Magick, Discoverie of Witchcraft.*"

His eyes flicked open and he said, "Yes, that's the one. Scot's *Discoverie of Witchcraft.* I'll think you'll find it's on the shelf just behind you, Dr. Watson."

I turned around and gazed at the tower of books behind me but could not see it. I moved closer and trailed my hand along the volumes. Suddenly Stone said, "That's the one!" It bore no

133

markings on the spine that I could see. I pulled it from the shelf and brushed the dust from the cover to reveal the title, *The Discoverie of Witchcraft*, and beneath that the name of the author, Reginald Scot.

"I think you'll find what you're looking for in book twelve under the heading, 'Another Way to Find out a Thief.' Only it will be written in old English, of course."

I thumbed through the stiff pages, fearful that I should tear them, and discovered that the text was indeed subdivided into books, the twelfth of which was devoted to charms against rogues and vagabonds. There it was, as Jacob had predicted, 'another wai to find out a theefe'. Holmes could see the look of incredulity on my face.

"Remarkable, is he not?" said my detective friend, delighting in my astonishment. "He never forgets anything he has read and he has read nearly everything."

"You flatter me, Holmes. I wish my mind was better attuned to more practical matters. I have yet to remember my wife's birthday correctly and I once forgot Christmas. At least I think it was once. My wife would probably tell you different. Never mind, is that what you are looking for, Dr. Watson?"

It was indeed. The book described a device identical to the one that Dr. Schermann was advocating. A finger ring tied to a length of thread would sway to indicate the identity of a thief. I handed the book to Holmes so that he could read it.

"And why exactly is this book banned?" I asked.

"Oh, it's no longer on the banned list but it is now so scarce that it is safer here than on the public shelves. It was written in the sixteenth century, at the height of the witch trials. Its author was a magistrate and the book is a sceptical one, pointing out that there is no such thing as magic and that witches are little more than deluded individuals persecuted out of ignorance. On that basis he advised the king to stop burning them."

"Really, and what effect did the book have?"

"None at all. The king burnt the book too. That's why it's rare."

Holmes closed the dusty volume and handed it to Jacob who tossed it onto the nearest shelf though, I noted, not the one I had taken it from.

"What else do you know about this device, Jacob? Does it actually work?" asked Holmes.

"Yes and no. Faraday did some work on table tipping and séance room phenomena – you might recall it – and discovered that muscular action was responsible for much of it. A person might push a glass across a table, spelling out a familiar name on an Ouija board without being aware that it is his own unconscious thought being manifested rather than a message from the spirit. Water dowsing is similar. So too is the pendulum."

"I recall Faraday's research," said Holmes, "But if the pendulum only reveals what the operator already knows, how could it help in the solving of a crime?"

"Psychology, Holmes, pure psychology. Give the pendulum to a guilty man and it may betray him. It is very like another ancient way of uncovering a criminal – medieval, I think. The suspect was interrogated and then asked to eat a morsel of cheese. If he could not swallow it, he was found guilty. Many people thought the story to be mere folklore but in fact it is founded on science. The mouth of a guilty man, having much to fear and battling against his own nerves, would quickly become dry. Swallowing the cheese could prove well nigh impossible."

"But I can see a drawback."

"Indeed. Habitual criminals are experienced lie tellers. I dare say that one would have no trouble beating the pendulum. Worse still, the pendulum amplifies our unconscious, and there lies the greatest trouble, for we are filled with prejudices. The pendulum will find whatever it is we wish to seek whether it is there or not."

"You're a good man, Jacob."

"A remarkable man," said I.

"You have told us more than I could have hoped for." Holmes patted him gently on the shoulder, raising some more dust into the bargain. "If you ever need my assistance you have only to call."

"While it would be good to watch you work, Holmes, I'm glad that so far I've never required your services. I hope I never shall, no offence meant."

"None taken," said Holmes.

"On the other hand if you can remember my wife's birthday or even find the shopping list that I have lost, well, there you can be of some use," said Stone amused by his own forgetfulness.

Holmes and I looked at Jacob Stone's paper festooned hat and both burst into laughter. Holmes reached forward, plucked the grocery list from its pin and then pretended to produce it from behind Stone's ear as a magician might produce a penny for a child.

"Don't let it be said that I ever kept a client waiting," said Holmes and once again laughter rang around the dusty room.

Chapter Twenty

I hardly slept that night and when I did I had the most frightful dream. I saw myself in a long corridor, the walls of which were pressing in with malevolent intent. An icy mist filled the hall and seemed to grow thicker with every step I took. Eventually, it became so dense that I could hardly see my hand in front of my face. And then suddenly, as is the case with dreams, I found myself in an entirely different place, a library. I was standing on an upper floor, looking over a balcony into the reading room that was set out beneath me. Thin men in dark coats and tall hats sat perusing books in which nothing at all was written. They turned the empty pages in unison, producing a great tearing sound, deafening to the ears. As I watched from my high vantage point, the doors of the reading room slowly opened and a young lady wearing a green dress and a large hat walked in. Her footsteps echoed around the room but no one looked up from their books. She walked past the silent readers at their desks until she was directly below the balcony and only a few feet from where I stood. Somehow she sensed me and slowly looked up and stared in my direction. I could not see her eyes for she wore a veil, but I knew that she saw mine and felt the terror in my heart. Then she lowered her gaze and continued her walk directly beneath me, her footsteps fading into silence. Her presence had a catastrophic effect on me. My hands were gripping the balcony rail tightly and my heart pounded in my chest. I felt faint and the room below me stirred and swayed as if under water. I took a deep breath and with great effort drew my gaze from this delirium and turned to walk away. And then I screamed. For there before me was the lady; the Mayfair murderer herself, her hands outstretched as if to grip my throat, a wide evil grin beneath her veil.

I awoke with a yell and soon heard Holmes pounding at my bedroom door.

"What is it, Watson?"

"Just a dream," I called. "Just a dream." I reassured him that everything was fine and begged him to go back to bed. I wish I could have taken my own advice but the thought of closing my eyes and seeing the apparition of the lady in green once again was too much. Instead, I got up and occupied my mind in other ways, reading a book and making some notes in my journal. It was some hours before daylight came but when it arrived it was most welcome. I looked out of my window upon the grey mist that swirled down Baker Street and found my mind still filled with dread. I had intended to go out and buy a newspaper but I could not shake off the phantasm I had seen in my dream. Instead I made up the fire in the sitting room and asked Mrs. Hudson for an early breakfast. By the time Holmes awoke I was feeling much better and ready for the day ahead, green lady and foggy London notwithstanding.

Holmes was in fine fettle, having consumed little breakfast but managing a cup or two of coffee. He had sent young Thomas for the newspaper, and when it arrived Holmes chortled with delight. Sims's article was front-page news. It hailed Dr. Karl Schermann as a positive genius and predicted that he was within mere days of apprehending the killer that had stalked Mayfair's streets. The new pendulum device was discussed in great detail and its virtues extolled in no uncertain terms. Sims assured his readers that they had one thousand and one uses and that authorised copies would be manufactured and made available to the general public at some point in the future. He noted that prices would be well within the pocket of those desirous of education in these matters. Messrs. Gamages had been appointed chief distributor.

More importantly, Sims hinted at a clue that made solving the murder case almost a formality. I assume he meant the sample of handwriting, evidence that had hitherto been kept from the pubic. The great and the good, led by Lady Bradford, heaped lavish praise on Dr. Schermann and said that they expected the case to be resolved very shortly. A dinner would be held in his honour at the Langham Hotel tonight. I noted that Lestrade's comments were more muted, saying merely that he 'hoped' the criminal would soon be brought to justice. Holmes had, as promised, provided a comment of his own. It was highlighted in bold type so that no one could fail to miss it. Dr. Schermann may be a subject of topical conversation but Holmes's reputation as a detective was unequalled:

'I feel sure that Dr. Schermann will indeed come upon the perpetrator of the foul deeds in Mayfair, and I only hope that I am there to see it.'
Sherlock Holmes

Anyone who did not know Holmes's ways might think of it as a recommendation. He glanced at the paper as I read it.

"Isn't that a hostage to fortune?" I asked, indicating the quotation.

"Not really, it means whatever you take it to mean. Sims believes one thing, I another."

"Then why give a statement at all?"

"Because I believe it will mean most to the very person we are seeking, the Mayfair murderer. Put yourself in the murderer's position, Watson. You are under a compulsion to kill. That is your nature. There is nothing you can do about it. You will kill again, you know that. You also know that the more you kill the greater the risk of getting caught. Now consider this. Who is the person most likely to catch you?"

"Yourself, Sherlock Holmes of course?"

"Not any more, Watson. You forget we have a new detective in the city, Dr. Schermann. Why, if the papers are to be believed, even the great Sherlock Holmes is in admiration of the fellow. Dr. Schermann is the man to beware of. Is he not being honoured by one of London's leading lights, the wife of the Commissioner of the Metropolitan Police no less?

"Yes, but I don't see where this is leading, Holmes."

"Perhaps you don't fully understand. Let me repeat. Our killer sits at home waiting for the next murderous moment. Fear of capture increases by the day. Dr. Schermann is on the trail. What would you do, Watson, if you were the murderer?"

Holmes held out his hands as if a great truth had been explained and handed over to me. How could I have been so blind? Holmes's plan was now obvious. He had spoken of laying a trap in the very papers the murderer used to snare her victims, and here it was on the front page. Sims's story and his nonsense about the psychic pendulum was the trap. Dr. Schermann was the bait!

"My word, Holmes, this a dangerous game you're playing."

"It's no game, my friend. It's been a matter of life and death since it began. I hope it will end soon. Now, where is my cherrywood pipe? It's time to consider our next move."

Holmes took the pipe from the mantelpiece, filled it and then took a seat by the fire. As the fine scent of tobacco wafted through our chambers he settled himself in his chair and meditated upon his actions. These were indeed high stakes, a foolish man's life used to trap a murderer. I wondered at the morality of it and considered whether my dear friend Holmes had let his vanity get the better of him. And then I doubted myself for having such traitorous thoughts. Holmes was my friend. If this was his plan, then I would support it. Five young women had already been killed and if it took extraordinary methods to capture their killer, then so be it. Silently, I hoped that I had made the right choice.

Chapter Twenty-One

Later that evening we had an unexpected visitor, Jacob Stone. He arrived breathlessly, a large book under his arm, his ancient stovepipe hat tilted at a precarious angle.

"Mr. Holmes, I am so glad to have caught you," he gasped, trying to catch his breath. He then slumped into a chair, exhausted. He had clearly been running and the heavy book had not made the activity any easier.

"Forgive me ... for calling on you ... without ... notice." He paused between the words, drawing in great gulps of air. "But I thought it ... important ... especially ... after ... reading ... today's ..."

"Newspaper?" interrupted Holmes.

"That's ... right." He handed the book to Holmes who took it eagerly. A paper strip projected from its pages and Holmes opened it at that point.

"Would you like something to drink, a brandy perhaps?" I offered. Jacob Stone nodded weakly and I poured him a glass, which he took in shaking hands. Holmes read the marked page, which seemed to me to consist of mathematical tables of some sort. His eyes seemed positively alive with excitement.

"Absolutely marvellous, Jacob. You are indeed the most remarkable archivist I have ever known."

Jacob raised his glass and straightened his hat. He had at last recovered some of his composure.

"I must look a state but I couldn't get a cab. The fog is thicker than ever and the streets deserted. But I just had to show you what I had found."

"I'm very grateful, Jacob. It's a dreadful day and you must indeed be on some urgent business to make your way here under such trying circumstances. Please, take your time. Enjoy your brandy."

Jacob took a sip and then, having recovered sufficiently, began his explanation.

"It's the Mayfair murders, Mr. Holmes. You piqued my interest and I took it upon myself to collate the articles from the newspapers. I was glad I did for I discovered something most peculiar."

"And what would that be?" said Holmes.

"It was the dates: the 30th of December, 8th, 15th, 22nd and the 29th of January. When I saw them they seemed strangely familiar and I was right. Each one a week apart, well almost, as if they belonged on some uncertain calendar. And then it suddenly struck me. Oh, I had been a fool to miss it. There was nothing uncertain in their arrangement. The dates are as regular as clockwork but not a clock made by man ... it is the 'Clock of God'. Can you believe it gentlemen? The 'Clock of God'!"

His eyes widened as he repeated the phrase and he appeared excited to have solved some puzzle but, to be truthful, I had no idea of the significance of what he was saying. Holmes shook his hand by way of congratulations while I wondered how much longer my bafflement was to continue.

"Is one of you gentlemen going to enlighten me? What exactly is the 'Clock of God'?" I asked.

Holmes handed me the book, it was an astronomical almanac covering some decades, and I glanced at its pages as he spoke.

"Simply put, Watson, the 'Clock of God' is the natural calendar by which all time is measured. It is Nature herself and her infinite variety of cycles and rhythms from which we have constructed our calendars, dividing the year into seasons, months, weeks and days. You can set your watch by Mother Nature, Watson – indeed that is what we do."

The pages of the book were, as I had thought, divided into tables. A long column of dates was printed on the left and against each date was a small circle, some shaded, some not, giving them the appearance of small black and white buttons. I looked for meaning as Holmes continued his explanation.

"But our ancestors, Watson, had another way of reading the passing of time. They marked their days using the method illustrated in that almanac, believing it to signify both birth and death. They are the phases of the moon. Its life is marked by the numbers on the page before you."

I ran my finger down the left hand column and slowed when I reached December. There was the 30th and against it the small circle was labelled the 'Moon's First Quarter'. Then the second date, the 8th January and against it 'Full Moon.' The 15th, 22nd and 29th of January followed, each marking another quarter. The dates of the Mayfair murders were no unhappy accidents. Each was tied firmly to the waxing and waning of the moon.

I looked at the next date in the column, wondering how much time we had left before some other young lady was to be murdered. It was the 6th February.

"My God, Holmes!"

"Yes, I know, Watson. Today is the full moon."

Holmes went over to the curtains and drew them aside. A grey fog shifted slowly outside our windows, leaving oily traces on the glass. Even so, high in the sky was a large faint luminescence of a full moon staring blindly down at the empty streets.

I closed the book and placed it aside.

"Does this mean our killer is quite literally a lunatic?" I asked.

Jacob Stone put down his glass and took it upon himself to answer my question. "Oh, no, Dr. Watson. The idea that people are made mad by the moon is pure superstition. Folklore and poppycock!"

Holmes gazed out at the sky as if searching for an answer.

"That is true but only so far as it goes," said Holmes. "While the moon may have no actual influence a sufficiently disturbed mind may well believe otherwise."

"Yes," said I, "I believe lycanthropy is one example. A man believes he is a werewolf and howls when the moon is full. Telling him it is nonsense does nothing to alleviate his condition."

"Have you considered witchcraft?" said Jacob. "Moon worship is an ancient practice. According to pagan tradition the three faces of the Goddess, the Maiden, Mother and Crone, all correspond to the different phases of the moon. The murderer might believe he is enacting some pagan ritual."

"That is a very interesting idea, Jacob, and I will meditate upon it. But time is pressing and I'm afraid that Watson and I have much to do."

Jacob needed no further prompting. He drained the last of his brandy and made his way to the door.

"I will leave the almanac with you, Mr. Holmes; you may have further need of it," he said.

"Very kind of you," answered Holmes. "Would you like me to arrange a cab? I have some friends nearby who I'm sure will be able to take you, the weather notwithstanding. I take it you are returning home?

"No, back to the Museum. I have much to do. I made my way here on foot and I shall return the same way, though less hastily. I thank you for the brandy, gentlemen, and I wish you the best of luck with your endeavours."

And with that he took off his tall hat, bowed and waved us goodbye.

Holmes was in a pensive mood. He stared out of the window, his brow wrinkled in thought, and watched Jacob walking along Baker Street, his hat bobbing with each step until he disappeared into the grey mist. Then, saying nothing, he turned and walked to the mantelpiece where his cherrywood pipe lay. Filling it once again with tobacco he sat in his chair by the fire and contemplated his next move. I did not want to interrupt his thought and so occupied myself with the almanac on the table and wondered what kind of bad business we had made for ourselves and how much worse it would get. I had much upon my mind but I knew that my friend Holmes had even more. And so I kept my council and awaited the result of his meditations. Suddenly, he spoke.

"Watson, this whole affair is shot through with superstition from beginning to end. First Schermann, and now our murderer. It is like a contagion, spreading from one to the other. We must not be drawn in or we shall be no better for it."

"Then what can we do?"

"Well, the first thing is that we must not concern ourselves with the motives of our murderer. To be perfectly honest, I am not the least bit interested in what the murderer believes himself to be, whether it is a witch, a werewolf or a three-faced Goddess. Let the hangman deal with them all. No, all we require is that our fiend acts upon his belief and attempts to carry out the next assault tonight."

"Holmes, you talk as if you want the murderer to continue."

"It is inevitable, Watson. Why would the murderer stop now? We must act while we have the advantage."

The smoke from his pipe mingled with the odour of Jacob's brandy in the most seductive way and our lodgings took on the atmosphere of a gentleman's club. Talk of murder, witchcraft, werewolves and lunacy seemed oddly out of place.

"Are you suggesting that we lie in wait along the streets of Mayfair and wait for the murderer to show up on the appointed date?"

"Not at all, Watson. You forget this morning's paper and Sims's article. If my calculations are correct, our murderer will take careful note of its contents and the next fatal appointment will not be with some unfortunate lady but with our own dear Dr. Shermann this very night."

"But where?"

"Wherever he happens to be. Didn't Sims say that he was to be honoured by Lady Bradford this evening?"

"Then we must inform the police," said I.

145

"And what will they do? They will put Dr. Schermann under guard and our murderer will take another victim instead, or perhaps decide to lie low until Dr. Schermann has moved on. And when he has left, the cycle will begin all over again. I'm afraid it is time for us to intercede. If the murderer is to make an attempt upon Dr. Shermann's life, then we must be there to apprehend them."

Holmes's strategy was risky but I could think of no other. The unsolved slayings of 'Jack the Ripper' ten years ago had left London uneasy and those fears had thrown both the police and the public into a panic when the murders in Mayfair began. That terror had given Dr. Schermann an opportunity to peddle his bogus theories, temporarily calming the public and providing them with fruitless hope. It had also set the police on a dark and dangerous road where superstition was the only light and what a dim and feeble light that was. This case had to have a resolution and it had to come quickly.

"Regrettably," I said, "you are right. Forewarning Dr. Schermann would serve little purpose."

"And if he is as psychic as he claims," said Holmes, "then shouldn't he already know what danger he is in?"

Holmes laughed, but I confess that I did not share his macabre humour. He sucked on his pipe and then blew out a large cloud of smoke that travelled the room like a grey spirit before slowly evaporating.

"Come, Watson, I hate to profit by a man's folly but I am of a mind that Dr. Schermann has brought this upon himself. I trust that I have not been equally foolish in setting forth so bold a plan."

"And when do we begin?" I asked.

"Immediately. It is time to pay our Dr. Schermann a visit and lay our cards upon the table. Let us pray we have the winning hand."

Chapter Twenty-Two

The fog was impenetrable and it was impossible to find a cab in Baker Street, so we walked to Joshua's, which was now full of drivers bemoaning how much money they were losing due to London's weather. Holmes spoke to Joshua and several of the cabbies at some length while I wrote a note for Inspector Lestrade, telling him of our intentions. Joshua took the note and 'Billy Three Coats' was persuaded to take us to Dr. Shermann's residence. It was a slow and treacherous drive and we met little else on the journey. Occasionally we would encounter another brave cabbie and 'Billy Three Coats' would give him a hearty shout. One of them was 'Tommy Tin Whistle', his cab empty and now on his way to Joshua's. He gave a couple of cheerful toots on his whistle as he went by.

Until we arrived at Grosvenor Square I had not realised that Dr. Schermann's house was located in Mayfair, haunt of our murderer. It was a fine dwelling, some four floors high, with long narrow windows, the upper tiers of which were guarded by iron-railed balconies, and a large pillared entrance that surrounded an imposing black oak door. 'Billy Three Coats' parked his cab and tended his horse while we walked the few steps to the door and rang the bell. We waited for what seemed an unnatural length of time, and so Holmes rang the bell again. We could hear voices within and then footsteps. The door opened and a tall cadaverous looking butler informed us that Dr. Shermann was not at home. He was about to close the door, apparently satisfied that he answered our enquiry, but Holmes pushed his hand against it and questioned him further.

"Then where may we find him?"

"I'm afraid it's not for me to say, sir," replied the butler with obvious indifference.

"My good fellow, my name is Sherlock Holmes and this is Dr. Watson. We must see Dr. Schermann as soon as possible. It is a matter of great urgency. Now let me restate my question and let us see if you can think of a better reply. Where is Dr. Schermann?"

The butler lowered his eyes, mumbled something that we could not hear and began to close the door once again. Holmes pressed hard against it and flung it open. It struck the wall with a great bang and the butler fell back onto the floor, shocked, his thin face pale and bloodless.

"I must insist," said Holmes, "You do your master no favours by obstructing us. Now where is Dr. Schermann?"

The frightened butler picked himself up and was about to make some answer when a voice called from inside.

"Let them in, Chivers."

It was Dr. Shermann himself, walking down the stairs at the end of the hallway. He wore a dressing gown and his wiry hair was strewn about his head like hay turned by the wind. It appeared that we had woken him from a nap. He took a pair of spectacles from his pocket and put them on.

"I am extremely sorry gentleman. You have my apologies. I had asked Chivers not to disturb me and, as you can see, he took his duties seriously."

He turned to his butler and asked him to bring some tea to the drawing room.

"That will not be necessary," said Holmes. "This is not a social call. I'm afraid we bring disturbing news."

Dr. Shermann led us into a magnificent drawing room, richly furnished and hung with expensive tapestries and bright landscapes. Its decoration was ostentatious in the extreme. Scarlet gold trimmed velvet cushions were scattered around the furniture. Roman busts, mounted on pillars, guarded the room's corners while a collection of porcelain figurines looked down from a high ornate fireplace. Overhead hung a splendid chandelier; its faceted glass throwing off glints of light. Life for a fortune-teller did not seem to be too hard.

"Not one stick of it is mine, gentleman," he said, guessing my thoughts.

"I take it the house belongs to Lady Bradford?" said Holmes.

"The butler also. And the maid and the cook. Everything. It is with Lady Bradford's most generous hospitality that I stay here. Please, sirs, do not ... how do you say ... stand on ceremony; take a seat and tell me how I may help you."

"Help us? I'm afraid you do not understand. It is we who have come to help you," said Holmes, startled by Dr. Schermann's offer.

"But, as you can see, I need no help." Dr. Schermann basked in the splendour that surrounded him, like one of the forty thieves who had stumbled upon Aladdin's cave. "Are you sure you would not like some tea?" he asked.

Holmes ignored Schermann's request and walked over to the fireplace where he studied the porcelain figures. His fingers touched them gently as a connoisseur might and then he picked one up turning it in his hand. He pulled out his glass for a closer look.

"This is a fake," he said. "I wonder if Lady Bradford knows she has a fake in her house? I take it she is no expert?"

"And you are, Mr. Holmes?"

"When it comes to porcelain, no. When it comes to fakes, yes." He threw the statuette towards Dr. Schermann who caught it against his chest. "Now do you want my help or not?"

Schermann placed the figure aside and pulled a bell rope to summon his butler. "Mr. Holmes, you talk in riddles. What is it you want? Please speak frankly and quickly, I have an appointment with Lady Bradford and I should hate to miss it. The aristocracy appreciate those who are punctual."

The butler arrived so quickly that I believe he must have been standing directly outside the door all this time, perhaps expecting further trouble. Dr. Schermann ordered his tea and Chivers left to fetch it. It was time for Holmes to play the cards he had been dealt and he began by telling Dr. Schermann exactly what he thought of his methods.

"Like the figure on that table, you, sir, are a fake of the first order. I have watched you ply your trade on the Continent, seducing the gullible with your superstition and charlatanry. But we have no time for your nonsense now. Your pendulum will aid no one, not the police nor yourself. It will merely give hope to the hopeless and I dare say you will be on your way to some foreign land before Lady Bradford realises what a shallow investment you have been. I come here for one reason only, and that is to tell you that you are in danger."

At the mention of danger to his own person, Dr. Schermann's pretence of indifference was broken and his curiosity piqued.

"Ah, I see I have your attention," said Holmes. "Did you, by the way, see the article in today's *The Times*?"

Schermann was surprised by the apparent change of direction in the conversation.

"Yes, I saw it," he answered, adding, "I thought it very good. I took your own view of my powers as a compliment."

"Then you took it wrongly. No doubt the murderer will do the same."

"The murderer?"

"Yes, the murderer reads the papers too. That very paper to be precise. That is where the young victims advertised for companionship. The murderer answered their enquiries, met them and slew them."

"Yes, I heard that from Inspector Lestrade. But I do not understand why that should affect me."

"It is simply this. There is but one man in London that can stop the murderer. Let's assume for the moment that that one man is you … this is purely hypothetical, of course."

"Of course," said Dr. Schermann, smiling at what he took to be flattery.

"Scotland Yard believes this to be true. Lady Bradford and Mr. George Sims believe this to be true. There is also one other that believes this to be true."

"I take it that is not yourself?"

"For once you are correct. No, the remaining person is, as it happens, the most important person of all, the murderer."

A loud knock at the door made Dr. Schermann jump. It was Chivers with his master's tea. Schermann sat down, no longer able to disguise his nervousness. He now knew where Holmes was leading him and it was not a place he wanted to go. He felt trapped, just as my friend had intended. Holmes said nothing until after Chivers poured the tea and departed. Schermann did not touch it; his mind now turned at last to more important matters, himself.

"Do drink your tea," said Holmes.

"Yes, yes. Please continue, Mr. Holmes. Your discourse is most fascinating."

"I think I have said all there is to say. Perhaps we should leave you to your tea. You say you have an appointment with Lady Bradford. I'm sure she would not want to be kept waiting."

Holmes started to leave and I with him but we had barely reached the door when Schermann called out to us.

"Please, we have begun on the wrong feet," he said, his German mangling the English a little. "Sit down, please."

There was an unmistakable note of fear in his voice. His bravado and boastfulness had disappeared leaving a shrunken figure of a man in its place. He knew the full implications of Holmes's message, that he would be the next victim of the Mayfair murderer.

"I'm sure the police will protect you," said Holmes.

But of course, Schermann knew that the police had been powerless to protect the five women who had already died.

"And you do have your psychic pendulum. I'm sure that is very reassuring in such frightful times."

Holmes was enjoying his moment and I could not deny it him. Schermann was everything that Holmes despised; an ignorant merchant of foolishness who took much and delivered nothing. In his way he was every bit as guilty as the murderer. If Holmes had been involved earlier perhaps one or two young lives could have been saved. Schermann's psychic nonsense had condemned them to death.

Schermann ignored his tea and turned to me for help, wondering if I could remain a witness to his dangerous situation and remain unmoved.

"Dr. Watson, I do not understand. Your friend is threatening me, is he not?"

"No," I said, "not threatening, merely informing. Holmes has told you the truth and I would have thought you would be grateful. The newspapers proclaim you a hero, the only man who can catch the Mayfair murderer. Surely you cannot expect the murderer to sit idly by while you formulate your plans. No, Holmes is right, the murderer will have you in her sights now."

"You might ask Lestrade to post a guard outside your door," said Holmes in mock helpfulness. "Still, it won't look good to the press. I don't know what Sims will think of you cowering inside while an assassin roams the streets. What do you say, Watson?"

"Oh, I agree entirely, Holmes. And I can't see that Lady Bradford would be too pleased either. Can't do a Lady's reputation much good to have a coward lodging in her house."

Schermann's wiry topped head was now gripped between his hands as if he had a monstrous headache. Holmes picked up the untouched cup of tea and gently forced it into his hand.

"What you need is a good cup of tea. Earl Grey, if I am not mistaken. Here, it will calm the nerves. Isn't that right, Watson?"

"Most certainly," said I.

"There you are, and as he is a real doctor you might want to consider his advice carefully, just as I am a real detective and therefore you might want to note what I am about to say."

Schermann raised his head. His eyes were moist as if he might burst into tears at any moment and his mouth drooped in the fashion of an idiot, his lower lip trembling uncontrollably. He sipped the tea and waited to be told what to do next as Holmes took the seat beside him.

"Make no mistake. You are in the most deadly danger. You are all that stands between the killer and freedom."

"Then I must leave," said Schermann quietly.

"On the contrary, you must stay, at least for a while. Then, when the killer is caught, you may go."

"No, I will leave today."

"What, and be remembered as a coward? Your career as a psychic will be at an end. No country in Europe will have you if you leave London in shame. Your patron Lady Bradford has many friends on the Continent. She may even persuade her husband to have you arrested."

"For what? I have done nothing."

"You have done much. I know about the little trick you pulled at the British Museum and I think that with a little help from the Royal Society I might be able to demonstrate that your psychic pendulum is a simple sham."

"No one will believe you."

"They will if they discover that their hero is trying to leave the country without lifting a finger to capture the murderer. No, you must stay here and help put right the wrongs you have set in motion. I insist."

He said it as if there were no alternative. With Lestrade's help Holmes could damage Schermann's reputation beyond repair but that was not the goal he had in mind. The Mayfair murderer had to be caught: only that would bring an end to the nightmare that had embraced London. What

153

happened to Schermann afterwards was of little concern to Holmes.

Schermann sat with a frozen gaze upon his face, the teacup just inches from his mouth, his red lined eyes aging him beyond his years. The fear that had welled up inside him now manifested itself as a tear, which slowly crept down his cheek. His world had been destroyed and now lay in ruins. It would never be the same for him in London, that much he knew. The fickle city had turned its back on Holmes and paid a dear price. It would just as quickly do the same to Schermann. However, this time it would be all the better for it. He set the cup aside and wiped his face on the sleeve of his dressing gown.

"I am sorry, Mr. Holmes."

"Sorry for yourself, that much I don't doubt. I don't require your apologies, Schermann, just your cooperation. Do I have it?"

"Yes. Anything."

"Then summon that servant of yours, I have a task for him."

Schermann pushed himself up from the chair and shuffled over to the bell rope that hung against the wall.

"Well, hurry, man. I'm afraid we don't have much time, you're to be murdered tonight!"

Upon hearing this Schermann fell into a faint and dropped to the floor like a stone, tugging the rope as he did so. The bell rang harshly throughout the house and a few moments later Chivers appeared at the door glaring at us both.

"I think the tea was too much for him," said Holmes pointing to Schermann as he lay upon the floor, the bell rope swinging idly above him. "Perhaps some smelling salts would be better! Do you have some?"

For a moment Chivers stood motionless, his mind racing to make sense of the bizarre scene that confronted him. Then he turned without saying a word and left to fetch the salts. I knelt beside the prone Dr. Schermann and measured his pulse. His eyelids were already flickering open and I knew he would shortly regain consciousness.

"Do you think she will take the bait," I said.

"She?" asked Holmes.

"The murderer."

"Ah, perhaps I have misled you there, my dear Watson. The murderer is no woman."

"Not a woman? But I thought ..."

Dr. Schermann was beginning to come around and Holmes interrupted me before I could question him further.

"I'll explain everything later, my friend. First, let's get Dr. Schermann back on his feet and then I'll be glad to tell you everything I know."

Holmes was once again master of the situation, commanding those around him like a general at the head of an army. Would London at last have the resolution it deserved? I checked my pocket watch and saw that it was already six o'clock and there was only an hour to go before Shermann's engagement with Lady Bradford. There was so much to do, and yet so little time to do it in, and I wondered whether anyone might accomplish it all in one night. The 'Clock of God' stops for no man, not even the great Sherlock Holmes.

Chapter Twenty-Three

Chivers tried to help Schermann by wafting some smelling salts under his nose but the bogus doctor pushed him away and, with some effort, picked himself up off the floor, determined to retain some shred of dignity. He retired to his bedroom to dress having resolved that he should, for his own benefit, be party to Holmes's plan. As soon as we were alone I questioned Holmes about the remark he had made earlier.

"What do you mean the murderer is not a woman? I thought that Lestrade said there had been several witnesses to that effect."

"Indeed," said Holmes, "but it was the witness statements that convinced me the opposite to be true. The murderer is a man, I am sure of it."

"How so?" said I.

"Do you remember what those witnesses saw?"

"Very clearly, I've had nightmares about it ever since," I said, referring to the night I awoke from a bad dream. "Each of them saw a lady dressed in green, wearing a hat and a veil, a fur stole and gloves. The hat bore a feather, or not, depending on which witness one chooses to believe, but aside from that they all gave the same description."

"And yet this description flies in the face of what we know to be true, that murderers are usually men and that in this case the murderer needed some considerable strength, a strength rarely found in women, since all his victims were strangled."

"I still don't see what makes you suspicious of the witnesses' descriptions."

"It's a very silly thing actually," said Holmes, "and it may well be I am wrong, but I find it difficult to believe that any woman, especially one as well dressed as our suspect, would wear the same attire on every occasion. Doesn't it seem strange to you that she always wore exactly the same green skirt and hat, gloves and stole? Only the feather is in dispute."

I was about to tell Holmes that his supposition was composed of the flimsiest of material and that his past experience of womankind hardly qualified him as an expert on their manner of dress. Then I thought of the women I had known and their almost fanatical obsession with fashion. Of course, none of them were murderers, at least to my knowledge. But the more I thought about them the more likely Holmes's conclusion appeared to be. It was indeed peculiar that our murderess only had one mode of dress.

"Your suggestion puts the case in an entirely different light," I said.

"I know. If our murderer is male, he entraps his victims by pretending to be female. The dress is no more than a disguise, the veil concealing his face, the gloves his hands. As to his motives I have no idea."

"Then there may be some psychotic sexual impulse at work."

"On that I refuse to be drawn. Transvestism is not my field of study. There are of course many cases on record of women posing as men and I dare say the opposite is also true. You might recall Catalina de Erauso or Mary Ann Talbot who spent generous amounts of their time impersonating the male gender. And there was the much-publicised case of Abigail Naylor who worked in a shipyard as a labourer and later married under the name of James Allen. I believe she played a fine game of billiards too. We shall know more when we capture our quarry but for now it would be prudent to assume that our lady in green is more than she appears."

When Schermann made an appearance he looked much calmer and had recovered much of his energy. Chivers brought him his coat and we left, exchanging the comfort of Schermann's home for the fog of the city and climbed into the carriage stewarded by 'Billy Three Coats'.

"I am cooperating because I want to, gentlemen," said Schermann as we drove to the Langham Hotel.

"Of course you are," said Holmes, "I had assumed nothing else."

"And when this evening is over, what will happen then?"

"That is entirely up to you, Dr. Schermann. What would you like to happen?"

"I would like to leave England. The weather here is unbearable."

"Then we certainly won't stand in your way, will we, Watson?"

"No at all," I said. "You'll miss the spring though, we have wonderful springs in England. It is the jewel of our year."

"I'm sure it is but it may not be quite the season you imagine when viewed from behind prison bars. And if my stay is extended I might not like the surroundings in which I find myself. Am I right, Mr. Holmes?"

"I'm afraid so. Inspector Lestrade has many questions. He has not taken well to Lady Bradford determining the future of our police force. I suspect that if we are successful tonight, an inquiry will be held. You may not want to be around for such an event."

"Then I will play my part tonight to the best of my ability, gentlemen. I used to be an actor, in Berlin. That was before I discovered my psychic talent."

"And what particular talent is that?" I asked.

"I know what people want, Dr. Watson. They want to believe. They want hope for their future."

"You give them false hope."

"False hope is better than no hope at all, is it not?"

"Then why not put your theory to the test, stay in England and hope for the best," I said. We heard no more from Schermann after that. Ten minutes later and the slow drive had brought us to the Langham Hotel close. It was a blaze of light in the darkness. A line of coaches and carriages stood silhouetted against the bright windows dispensing elegantly dressed ladies and gentlemen onto the pavement. Doormen ran out to greet them and usher them inside. We said goodbye to Schermann and watched him walked into the hotel, and when he was lost from view Holmes shouted to 'Billy Three Coats' and asked him to park the carriage across the road. And then we waited.

Chapter Twenty-Four

We counted the great and the good as they entered Langham's portals. Lady Bradford certainly had a most impressive collection of acquaintances, and that they should turn out on such an inhospitable night was a tribute to the influence she held in society. I noted that one of those guests was Inspector Lestrade, and hoped that he had received the note from Joshua requesting his cooperation. He looked very dapper in his dinner jacket, and I commented upon the fact to my friend. George Sims was also there and a flattering account of the evening would no doubt appear in *The Times* or *The Sunday Referee*.

If Holmes's theory was correct and Schermann was the next intended victim of the Mayfair murderer, then he couldn't have been in a safer place than in the company of Lady Bradford's friends. Half of Scotland Yard's officers must have been among them, dining in the warmth of the Langham while the other half kept watch in Mayfair, hoping to apprehend the murderer.

By eight o'clock all the guests had arrived and the doormen had closed the hotel doors. Some of the carriages, like our own, stayed parked in the surrounding streets, their drivers gathering together to talk, and smoke and generally pass the time. 'Billy Three Coats' stayed at his post, perched there like a grey gargoyle. A flask of brandy or some other spirit kept him warm and occasionally he would call down to us with some comment. I wished I had thought to bring some of my own.

Holmes left our carriage to go on a reconnaissance. Although the fog was still thick, the lights of the Langham gave out sufficient illumination to enable me to watch him walk the ten yards or so to the hotel. He went inside and stayed there for some time. Without Holmes to talk to, the waiting seemed interminable and I could feel the winter cold slowly creeping into my bones. I stamped my feet and rubbed my hands to keep them warm, and I realised how wise 'Billy Three Coats' had been in adopting his eccentric dressing habits. I checked my pocket watch numerous times but the hands of it hardly seemed to change between one look and another. I shook it, thinking that perhaps the mechanism had stopped, frozen by the wintry cold. But it hadn't and the watch ticked merrily on unhurried by my impatience. I was checking it again when the carriage door opened and Holmes climbed inside.

"Keeping a watchful eye open I see," said Holmes.

"Just wondered what the time was. I was becoming a little concerned."

"Not to worry. Schermann is alive and well and enjoying his main course. Fish I believe and jolly good it looked too. According to the hotel manager the dinner finishes at ten-thirty, I don't suppose much will happen until then."

Holmes sat opposite me and withdrew a small bottle and two glasses from his pocket.

"I thought this might keep the chill at bay."

He poured us both a nip of brandy and we once again took turns at the carriage window, watching the streets and the fog that flowed through them.

It was eleven o'clock by the time the first guests began to emerge from the hotel and make their way to their carriages. Hansoms, broughams and growlers vied for the prime spot before the hotel door as they collected their passengers. The guests' arrival may have been orderly but their departure was anything but as they wandered into the fog, calling for their drivers. Within minutes a melee was under way as carriages and horses frantically tried to take their leave. Drivers who had moments earlier been enjoying a friendly chat were suddenly exchanging insults in the fog. We told 'Billy Three Coats' to take his place in the untidy parade and pick up Dr. Schermann. The plan was for Billy to meet us further down the street, and then we would all travel together to Schermann's house in Grosvenor Square and keep an eye out for anyone that might follow.

We had no sooner stepped onto the pavement than I heard the loud rattle of wheels as a cab pulled up beside us. The driver shouted down to Holmes.

"Mr. Holmes, Mr. Holmes. It's Tommy, they found him unconscious." I recognised the driver as one of the men I had seen at Joshua's. It was 'Sweet Apple Joe'.

"'Tommy Tin Whistle'?" said Holmes.

"The very same. Left for dead he was and his horse and cab stolen. Joshua said I should tell you immediately."

"Is Tommy all right?" I asked.

"Alive and lucky to be so I'd say. His thick skull came in handy after all."

I looked to Holmes for the significance of this news but he was already running across the road towards the hotel. I followed, dodging between the horses and carriages and apologising to the waiting ladies and gentlemen and anyone else who came in my way.

"Watson, find Schermann," shouted Holmes as he saw me following him.

It was no easy matter. What the fog didn't hide, the chaos did and after a fruitless search I made my way to the hotel doors and waited for Holmes's return. To my surprise he emerged from the hotel itself.

"He's not here," said Holmes.

"Not here? Then where is he?"

At that moment 'Sweet Apple Joe' drew his carriage up beside us.

"That's Tommy's horse and cab," he said, pointing to a shadow in the fog.

"Quick, man, get inside," said Holmes. "Do you think you can follow him, Joe?"

"If I can't no one else can," said Joe and before we could close the door the cab was moving.

As we set off, Holmes leaned out of the window and called to Billy, "Tell Inspector Lestrade what has happened. Dr. Schermann has been kidnapped."

That much was obvious. Schermann had climbed into the first carriage that offered to take him. Our quarry had now taken the lead and we had no choice but to pursue him. Dr. Schermann's carriage sped into the fog at almost suicidal speed, and we followed, our cab rocking and rolling like a boat in a storm, the clattering of hooves as loud as thunder and the crack of the whip as sharp as lightning.

I leaned out of the window just as we entered Oxford Circus and held tight onto the door. We were but a few yards from the carriage ahead but I could not get a good look at the driver nor could I see Shermann through the carriage window. But the sight of that carriage racing into the grey blank wall that the fog presented was terrifying in the extreme as was the knowledge that we were following in its demonic wake. The journey down Regent Street was the quickest I have ever known. It was a wild ride and no mistake.

I was about to pull my head inside when I thought I saw the strangest thing. It happened as we entered Piccadilly Circus, the carriage tilting at a precarious angle. For there, faintly illuminated by a streetlight, I saw another carriage, an open topped brougham. And as we sped by I thought I saw the driver wave at me, as if signalling to a ship at sea. I did not know what to think of it. Once inside the carriage I turned to Holmes but he was busy looking out of the other window. And so I looked out of my window again but by the time I did, the brougham was gone and we were heading down Piccadilly. It was just a few streets away from here that the Mayfair murders began and I pondered Holmes's comments about a murderer always returning to the scene of his crime. That ruinous habit had trapped Higson the jewel thief at

Cantle's auction room. Then I saw another carriage, this one waiting in Berkeley Street, and again its driver waved to me, or so I thought. This time I could not keep the information to myself, so I tugged at Holmes's coat and tried to make myself heard above the din and clatter of the ride.

"Holmes, there are carriages parked in the side streets!" I shouted.

"Indeed," said Holmes, "They are friends of Joshua. If my calculations are right our journey will soon be over. Take a look and hold on tight!"

Hyde Park Corner lay just ahead but when I popped my head outside the carriage I could, of course, see none of it. We had, however, gained on Dr. Schermann's carriage and managed to pull up alongside. I could see Schermann within, his mouth open, his eyes wide and in a state of utter shock. His arms were outstretched and pressed against either side of the cab in a desperate attempt to keep himself upright. Our cabs came dangerously close and then closer still until only a few inches separated them. I could hear the hubs of the wheels grind together and a violent shudder racked both carriages. I ducked my head inside and held on tightly, preparing for what I thought was the inevitable collision. Holmes too prepared himself for the worst. We raced side by side, the grinding getting louder but the collision never came. Schermann's cab unexpectedly changed course and pulled away to our right while ours continued straight ahead. Joe quickly brought our cab to a halt, though not without some effort, and I watched Dr. Schermann's disappear into the distance.

"We've lost him," I said.

"Not yet we haven't," replied Holmes, "but from here we go by foot."

Go by foot? The very idea seemed foolish but before I could question Holmes further he was out of the door and running after Dr. Schermann. As ever, I followed while Joe shouted something about using his cab to guard the way back. It was then that I saw a line of police carriages blocking the road ahead. The sudden change of direction had been no accident.

Holmes had surely told Lestrade of his plan and a cordon of police had already sealed off Mayfair in anticipation of another murder.

Holmes was but a faint shadow in front of me but I could still make out the barest illumination from the lantern of the cab we pursued. As far as I could determine we were heading along Hamilton Place and very soon would be in Park Lane. I could see the railings of Hyde Park to my left but beyond them lay a dark abyss where the absence of street lighting surrendered that part of London to the dank fog. Suddenly there was an almighty crash and the scream of horses. It shook me to the core and made me fearful of rushing any further into the darkness. But Holmes did not falter and so I, reluctantly, quickened my pace.

A broken wheel soon came into view, its spokes splintered, and ahead of that the carriage itself, fallen on its side like a dark wreck in the ocean. Blood pooled onto the road and I could see that one of the horses was down on the ground, badly injured and whinnying with pain. The scene was cast in an odd yellow light that came from a row of lanterns directly ahead of us. I had no idea what they where until I realised that they were moving ever closer. And then, from out of the fog, I saw six carriages, their lights blazing, side-by-side across the entire span of the road. It was Joshua and his friends and I knew then that they had been part of Holmes's master plan, following our chase from Langham Place and building a barricade ahead of us. The murderer had tried to bring his carriage to an abrupt halt and in doing so had turned it over. I walked around the broken cab but could see no one and knew that the murderer had already fled.

Holmes stood on the upended carriage and pulled open the door. He saw that Dr. Schermann was still inside and hauled him out, bruised and frightened but otherwise unharmed.

"Take care of him, Joshua," said Holmes, "this matter is not finished yet."

"Then take this," said Joshua, throwing him a pistol. Holmes weighed it in his hand and then tucked it into his coat pocket. "He ran across the park, through Stanhope Gate," he said, pointing to the stygian darkness beyond the railings.

"Are you ready for some more exercise, Watson?"

"I'd rather that than another cab ride," I said, and followed him through the gate that led into Hyde Park.

The fog grew worse. Without the streetlights, it was almost impenetrable and the moon that had somehow brought about this madness was our only guide. It was impossible to move with any speed for fear of smashing into some unseen obstacle and so we crept along crunching the gravel of the pathway beneath our feet, our stealth forced upon us but useful nonetheless. Our prey was faced with the same problem as ourselves and whenever we stopped we could hear him moving ahead of us. How far ahead, I could not say. My mind went back to the dreams I had been having and I imagined him suddenly bursting from the darkness his hands at my throat. It wasn't long ago that we found ourselves in a similar situation at Belle Tout Lighthouse, fighting our enemy in the dark.

Our pace had slowed to a crawl and our ears pricked at every snap of a twig or rustle of a dead leaf. I felt sure the murderer knew we were behind him, even now thinking what plans he might make to affect his escape. We followed wherever he led and as a result were soon taken from the gravel path onto the damp and frosted grass. Tracking him was more difficult now but at least we were able to quicken our pace. As we did, great leafless trees loomed out of the fog their bare and angular branches reaching out to us like great claws. I tried to recall where we might be but the park presented an alien landscape so different from the green space I had often strolled through during the summer. And then we heard a sound. We stopped and strained our eyes to look ahead. We could see nothing but just as we were about to move forward, we heard the sound again, a rustling of leaves along the ground. We stared into the darkness. Holmes drew his gun and pointed it ahead for what seemed an inordinate length of time. Watching, waiting. And suddenly there was a great commotion and something ran at us from out of the gloom. It struck my leg and I looked down astonished to see that it was a fox. It was as surprised as I and temporarily stunned by its collision. The fox gave me a quick glance and then shot off into the park, leaving as quickly as it had arrived. Holmes put the gun away and we continued our blind march, myself a little shaken by our nocturnal encounter.

We had been walking for some time when Holmes signalled to me and I drew close.

"He's heading for the Serpentine," whispered Holmes, "the bridge lies just before us and it's the only way across unless he fancies a swim. I'm going to go ahead. You stay back and make sure he doesn't decide to change his mind."

Holmes took the pistol from his pocket and pressed it into my hand. I didn't want to take it but Holmes insisted.

"You're a better shot than I, Watson. Take it."

So I did, and Holmes crept silently away into the fog. I noted that I could hardly hear him move, and it was mere seconds before he was out of sight. I walked on, more slowly, pistol in hand and ready to shoot should the wrong man make himself visible.

Silence, total silence and nothing to be seen. It was a rare experience to be deprived of both sight and hearing. The only method of navigation was by the faint light of the full moon, veiled by the murky vapours that cloaked London. Its illumination was of little use but its location in the heavens was the only point by which I could reckon my position. I followed Holmes as swiftly as I could, being careful not to signal my presence and upon reaching the bridge without incident, I decided to wait there. It was, as Holmes had said, the only way back across the water. It stood like a grey ghost in the darkness, its opposite end lost in the fog. It occurred to me that perhaps our murderer had not yet made the crossing and was still behind me. It was an idea that put fear into my heart and I turned this way and that in case he was about to jump out of the foggy darkness at me.

I do not know how long I waited there and for a while heard nothing save the gentle ripple of the water, which, although invisible in the darkness, was probably less than ten feet from me. I think the gentle sound had lulled me somewhat for when I next looked at the bridge I saw a figure upon it walking towards me. I wondered whether to call to verify that it was Holmes but then decided this hasty action would just make my presence known. The figure came closer and yet still I could not make out its features. I held the pistol steady, ready to shoot if necessary. I knew too that if I could see the figure, the figure could see me. My mind once again tumbled back to the dream of the green lady in the library. Step by step the figure came closer a surreal phantom in the mist.

"Watson, look out!"

It was Holmes. The figure ran towards me.

"Watson, look out!"

There was something strangely odd about the situation. Holmes's warning and the figure before me, at first my mind had connected the two but now I had my doubts. It was a split second before I realised what was wrong. The voice was Holmes's but the figure wasn't. It dashed towards me and struck me with all its weight, forcing me against the balustrade of the bridge. I felt its hands against my throat, its fingers strong and powerful, gripping like steel. I pushed back with all my might and then struck it a blow across the head with the barrel of the pistol. It shrieked in pain, fell back and then came at me again. This time I saw its face. It was the face of an angel on the head of a fiend. Its unnaturally pale skin was flawless, like a mask, stretched over high cheekbones and a sturdy chin. Its eyes were dark and guileless and I could readily see how he might have lured his victims to their deaths. Only a malevolent grin spoiled the visage, that and a gash I had opened on its forehead. He tried to take me by the throat again, growling like an animal as blood seeped down his face. I struck him a blow in the chest with my elbow and then another wallop with the pistol, which tore a deep scar across his angelic features. He quickly

169

loosened his grip and tried to turn and run. Unwittingly he ran straight into Holmes who had been following him and now sent the figure reeling with a well-aimed blow from his fist. Caught between us on the bridge he turned and snarled like an animal unsure which of us he should take on, Holmes with his fists or me with the pistol. He decided on neither and leapt onto the balustrade with the intention of throwing himself into the Serpentine. Quickly I aimed the pistol and fired. There was a flash as the shot rang out and a moment later the figure fell clutching his leg. As intended, I had wounded him in order to prevent his escape.

"Good shot, Watson! I knew you were the man to trust," said Holmes. He crouched down next to the figure to get a better look at our prisoner. The man was grimacing from pain and breathing heavily as blood poured from his leg.

"Perhaps you should fire another shot," said Holmes. With luck Joshua or someone might hear it. We're going to need some help to take him back.

Holmes took a handkerchief from his pocket and started to bind the wounded man's leg, while I raised the gun to fire a shot into the air. What happened next took but a few moments yet seemed at the time, and still seems now, to have taken an eternity.

My finger was on the trigger, the gun pointed towards the dim moon, and Holmes was tying a knot in the handkerchief. The blood blossomed on the white cotton like a dark rose. And then, behind Holmes's shoulder I saw a glint of light. Slowly it moved in the darkness, rising upwards until it was held still and motionless. The prisoner turned his head towards me as if wanting me to look at him and burn the tableau into my brain. He smiled, the blood from his head wounds dividing his face in two and gathering around his lips. Then the steel in his hands glinted again and he brought the knife down into Holmes's throat. At least that was what I saw. Or thought I saw. Because somehow I had brought the pistol down and fired off a shot before the blade struck my friend. The bullet burst open the demon's angel face and the knife fell to the floor. His legs twitched and what remained of his head fell back against the balustrade. Twin moons were reflected in his otherwise empty eyes.

Holmes did not flinch when I made the shot nor move until the incident was over. He picked up the knife from the floor and examined its blade, a blade that had nearly ended his life. Then he slipped it into his pocket and walked over to me. He put a hand on my shoulder and even now I find it difficult to put into words what he said to me that night. But I do remember this and it is something I have tried to live by ever since.

"Watson," he said, "I see I made the right decision."

"In giving me the gun?" I asked.

"No, in having you as a friend. I should thank you for my life. But I won't. Instead I will beg your forgiveness."

"For what?" I said.

"For not thanking you earlier. It is easy to thank someone after a favour has been done. But next time you might not be as quick and so I would like to thank you now, in advance as it were, for all that you have done and all that you will do. I have never had a finer friend, and I want you to know that for this one blessing I am eternally grateful."

I patted him on the back and told him that it didn't matter, but the fact was that it mattered very much. I fired another shot into the air and we soon heard the dull thud of hooves across the grass as several carriages drove into view. Joshua had found us and this time Lestrade was with him. He immediately jumped down from the cab and ran over to see what had happened.

"I take it this is the Mayfair murderer?" said the Inspector.

"I hope so," said I, "or it will be a mighty blot on our record, eh, Holmes?"

"You never fail to surprise me, Watson," he said laughing. "Time to bring this case to a close, Inspector. I trust you and your officers can attend to the rest."

There were many questions still to be answered but for now they could wait. Holmes and I had come to the end of our task. It was unfortunate that the suspect was dead; that had never been our intention, but not all problems can be resolved easily. We had done our best and that is all we can ever do.

Many of the more salacious details of the case were given in *The Sunday Referee*, courtesy of Mr. George Sims. He had accompanied the police when the murderer had been identified and his abode located. His name was Stefan Gregor, the dissolute son of a noble Russian family. In his house they found the green lady disguise, said to have once belonged to his fiancée whose body was later discovered in the cellar. She was his first victim and Sims told his readers that it was as a result of this killing that Stefan Gregor's mind became unhinged. However, Lestrade told us that while much of what Sims said was true, there was much that he left out. The house was lined with books on witchcraft and demonology and many other kinds of depraved literature. One room was locked and when they broke the door down they found what appeared to be a satanic altar inside. Gregor had also kept a meticulous and lurid journal of his assassinations, each of which he felt compelled to carry out at the bidding of his master, Satan. It was decided that its contents were too disturbing to be made known to the public and it was immediately consigned to a collection of criminal artefacts held in Scotland Yard's 'Black Museum'. Instead Scotland Yard were content for Sims to label the murderer as a lunatic. And the public seemed equally happy to believe it.

As for Dr. Schermann, he left London as he had promised and once again took up residence in Paris where he married a rich and elderly widow. If he was hoping to eventually profit by her death he was sadly mistaken. Dr. Schermann choked on a fishbone at a dinner given in his honour and his widow became even wealthier as a result of an insurance claim. If he had taken the trouble to note that she had profited and been widowed by two similar claims before, he might not have thought it a match worth making.

As Holmes had predicted, Lestrade persuaded the authorities to set up an inquiry into Scotland Yard's investigation of the Mayfair murders. Lady Bradford's role as her husband's advisor was curtailed and the use of psychics and other dubious consultants to help in police matters was banned. The solving of crimes was to be dealt with by those who had expertise in such matters. Holmes, of course, was counted amongst them and pleased to be mentioned by name in the official report. He was London's most celebrated detective, and following the Mayfair murders interest in his methods was never greater. And once again he found himself advising Her Majesty's Government on matters of national importance, an outcome that brought him great satisfaction despite his protestations to the contrary. He tackled his work with renewed vigour, finding the extraordinary in the commonplace and solutions where others saw only enigmas. That the Empire has benefited from his presence is surely not in doubt. As for myself, I try to chronicle each case as accurately as possible, pleased to share Holmes's adventures and confidences and proud to be called his friend. It is a task I am delighted to be charged with and I hope it will long continue. And any 'embellishments' I may be accused of adding are there for one reason only. They are all true!

"With five volumes you could fill that gap on that second shelf"
(Sherlock Holmes, *The Empty House*)

So why not collect all 44 murder mysteries from Baker Street Studios? Available from all good bookshops, or direct from the publisher with free UK postage & packing at just £7.50 each. Alternatively you can get full details of all our publications, including our range of audio books, and order on-line where you can also join our mailing list and see our latest special offers.

IN THE DEAD OF WINTER
MYSTERY OF A HANSOM CAB
SHERLOCK HOLMES AND THE ABBEY SCHOOL MYSTERY
SHERLOCK HOLMES AND THE ADLER PAPERS
SHERLOCK HOLMES AND THE BAKER STREET DOZEN
SHERLOCK HOLMES AND THE BOULEVARD ASSASSIN
SHERLOCK HOLMES AND THE CHILFORD RIPPER
SHERLOCK HOLMES AND THE CHINESE JUNK AFFAIR
SHERLOCK HOLMES AND THE CIRCUS OF FEAR
SHERLOCK HOLMES AND THE DISAPPEARING PRINCE
SHERLOCK HOLMES AND THE DISGRACED INSPECTOR
SHERLOCK HOLMES AND THE EGYPTIAN HALL ADVENTURE
SHERLOCK HOLMES AND THE FRIGHTENED GOLFER
SHERLOCK HOLMES AND THE GIANT'S HAND
SHERLOCK HOLMES AND THE GREYFRIARS SCHOOL MYSTERY
SHERLOCK HOLMES AND THE HAMMERFORD WILL
SHERLOCK HOLMES AND THE HILLDROP CRESCENT MYSTERY
SHERLOCK HOLMES AND THE HOLBORN EMPORIUM
SHERLOCK HOLMES AND THE HOUDINI BIRTHRIGHT
SHERLOCK HOLMES AND THE LONGACRE VAMPIRE
SHERLOCK HOLMES AND THE MAN WHO LOST HIMSELF
SHERLOCK HOLMES AND THE MORPHINE GAMBIT
SHERLOCK HOLMES AND THE SANDRINGHAM HOUSE MYSTERY
SHERLOCK HOLMES AND THE SECRET MISSION
SHERLOCK HOLMES AND THE SECRET SEVEN
SHERLOCK HOLMES AND THE TANDRIDGE HALL MYSTERY
SHERLOCK HOLMES AND THE TELEPHONE MURDER MYSTERY
SHERLOCK HOLMES AND THE THEATRE OF DEATH
SHERLOCK HOLMES AND THE THREE POISONED PAWNS
SHERLOCK HOLMES AND THE TITANIC TRAGEDY
SHERLOCK HOLMES AND THE TOMB OF TERROR
SHERLOCK HOLMES AND THE YULE-TIDE MYSTERY
SHERLOCK HOLMES: A DUEL WITH THE DEVIL
SHERLOCK HOLMES AT THE RAFFLES HOTEL
SHERLOCK HOLMES AT THE VARIETIES
SHERLOCK HOLMES ON THE WESTERN FRONT
SHERLOCK HOLMES: THE GHOST OF BAKER STREET
SPECIAL COMMISSION
THE ADVENTURE OF THE SPANISH DRUMS
THE CASE OF THE MISSING STRADIVARIUS (HARDBACK AT £15.99)
THE ELEMENTARY CASES OF SHERLOCK HOLMES
THE TORMENT OF SHERLOCK HOLMES
THE TRAVELS OF SHERLOCK HOLMES
WATSON'S LAST CASE

Baker Street Studios Limited, Endeavour House, 170 Woodland Road, Sawston, Cambridge CB22 3DX
www.breesebooks.com, sales@breesebooks.com